T0279073

MY
FAIRY GOD
SOMEBODY

Also by Charlene Allen
Play the Game

MY FAIRY GOD SOMEBODY

CHARLENE ALLEN

HARPER
An Imprint of HarperCollinsPublishers

Library of Congress Control Number: 2023948877
ISBN 978-0-06-321284-8

Typography by Joel Tippie
24 25 26 27 28 LBC 5 4 3 2 1

First Edition

For Roberta McCombs, aunt and matriarch, who told us the truth and taught us to fiercely honor both independence and connection

The great force of history comes from the fact that we carry it within us, are unconsciously controlled by it in many ways, and history is literally present in all that we do. It could scarcely be otherwise, since it is to history we owe our frames of reference, our identities, and our aspirations.
—James Baldwin

ONE

UNCLE WENDELL AND THE RING

Am I about to do this?

I close my bedroom door and press my back against it, shutting out the smell of baking crust, the sound of Mom's humming. And the stress of faking it with her all day. Warm light from my bedside lamp spills over the art supplies scattered on my quilt. It's maybe the fifth time I've come up here today, just to make sure what's real is real. And there it is, the edge of the plastic bin I shoved under the bed, peeking out like a promise. Nervous excitement sizzles from my stomach to my face. It's real.

I'm doing this.

I squat down and reach for the bin. Inside, under my winter boots, are two envelopes. I grab them, stand up, and empty the thicker one onto the quilt. Out comes a four-by-six photo, unframed. And a ring, emerald in a bronze setting

First, I pick up the photo and give it a kiss. Some people would think it's a sad picture, a middle-aged Black man standing by a cart in the mostly empty parking lot of the Stop & Shop. His arms hang loose, his hands too big for his wrists. A confused crease splits the middle of his forehead, and a shy smile bends his lips. My uncle Wendell, who people called slow, not all there—but who was there for me. Who was mostly not sad, at least when I was with him. Who was the only for-sure uncle I've ever had. My uncle Wendell, who gave me the emerald-and-bronze ring just two weeks ago. Right before he died.

The metal's cool to the touch as I scoop up the ring in my palm. An old, cold secret. Raised writing surrounds the dull green stone. *JM Smith High School, Bklyn NY: NEA ONNIM NO SUA A, OHU.* I know from the internet this means "He who does not know can know from learning," in some West African language. Inside the ring, the word *river* is inscribed. I have no idea what that means. But I know why Uncle Wendell gave me this ring. It was my dad's. It had to be.

My final treasure is in the other envelope. I touch it for reassurance. No need to actually read the letter inside, because I memorized it in the eight hours since I nabbed it from the mailbox. *Dear Ms. Mitchell . . . excited to welcome you to New York City!* And in the last line . . . *check enclosed.*

Soon, I will be going to New York. Where Uncle Wendell is leading me. Where my dad used to live. Where there are answers.

My phone buzzes. It's Roxy, who should be getting here any minute for one of Mom's famous dessert parties.

Roxy: Leaving now. Tell your mom sorry I'm late.

I write back:

Me: No worries. Pie's still in the oven.

Relieved to have a few more minutes, I put down the photo, grab my sketchbook off the desk, and rip out the used pages so it's as if it was brand-new. Now there's time to get started on my idea. My sketchbook's about to become an art project, vision board, and evidence wall, all in one. A way to make it all make sense.

Carefully, I tape the photo of Uncle Wendell on the first page of the sketchbook. This is, after all, thanks to him. He was in a talking mood that day in the parking lot. That whole visit, really. And the simplest thing led to a story.

"So, Uncle Wendell," I said, when he got excited about all the things in the store. "You don't have big grocery stores where you live?"

"Uh-uh," he said, emphasis on the first *uh*. And he broke into a story about the general store, back when he and Mom were kids in Virginia. He painted a picture with his soft drawl, making me see wooden rocking chairs on the porch of the store and old Black men smoking pipes. One of those old men could have been my grandpa, I imagined. And Uncle Wendell might've told me about him, except that Mom can't deal with the past. Even the part *before* my deadbeat dad. She'd turn up, like some kind of bat, feeling her way to the story and gobbling it up halfway out of Uncle Wendell's mouth.

"How would you know, Wendell?" she'd say. "All you ever did was watch television all day."

Uncle Wendell would say, "That's true, too. You ever looked at *Family Matters*?" And he'd tell *that* story, as if he'd been right there, inside the episodes.

He was our only relative, Mom and me. He hadn't just grown up with her in Virginia, he'd even lived in New York when my mom and dad met. He knew things, Uncle Wendell—things I needed to know.

I flip the page and add a heading:

Uncle Wendell and the Ring.
I want to capture the story so I never forget. Mom tried to warn me what cancer did to people. But I didn't get it till I saw Uncle Wendell being wheeled through the airport, his skin hanging off his long bones. The word I thought of was spent, *like he'd binge-shopped with all his life points during some crazy day at the mall. And there was only enough left to get him home.*

We gave him my room. I'd been sitting by the bed one day, ready with his lunch, when he woke up. That crease left his brow when he was sleeping, making him look even more like Mom: high cheekbones, warm brown skin, and those narrow, turned-down eyes. The opposite of me, with my darker skin, flat cheeks, and eyes that turn *up* at the edges. For the zillionth time, I thought, *I've gotta look like my dad's side.* And right then, Uncle Wendell started talking. Out of nowhere. Out of his dying all-over-the-place mind.

"I don't see that it's right," he said. Then he opened his eyes and settled them on me. "You, so lonesome."

I tried to tell him that I was fine, but he was in his own world and kept going.

"Truth is," he said. "You're not alone. People should know who all they belong to."

He reached into his pajama pocket and pulled out something.

4

I thought it was gonna be a nasty tissue, because what else could he have in there? But he eyed the door and said, "Don't tell your momma."

My heart beat louder than his rasping breath as I reached for what he held. A ring. Big and bronze and heavy in my hand. A man's ring.

"Is it something from before?" I asked. "Something to do with my dad?" The thought's never far, but I don't know why I asked it just then.

"Your daddy," he said. And he closed my fingers around the ring.

"My dad!" I said. "*Was this his?*"

But Uncle Wendell just lay there, breathing harder, worn out. I stared from him to the ring, thinking what to ask next, until his breathing changed, and I knew he was sleeping.

Before I could talk to him again, he was gone.

Now, I touch the ring, careful, like it's a tiny living thing. Evidence is what it is. Evidence that there's stuff worth knowing, even if my mom won't talk about it. Stuff Uncle Wendell wanted me to know.

I run my finger along the word *river* inside the ring, then lay it on the next page of the sketchbook and carefully trace it. I write *JM Smith HS* in a swirly line around it, wondering again why there's so little on the internet about it. I grab my phone and pull up the screenshot of a Wikipedia page I found that mentioned the school, and write what it says, word for word, in the scrapbook: *J. M. Smith High School, started in 1970 as part of a network of Black Freedom Schools, providing educational options outside the state system.*

Next to the school's name I write: *river?*

I finish the page with Uncle Wendell's words:

"People should know who all they belong to."

I've already planned the next two pages in my head. I need to put down everything I've thought about over the years that points in the same direction as what Uncle Wendell said. *I'm not alone.* I have *family*, on my dad's side. Somewhere in New York City.

First, I draw an open laptop—Mom's laptop on the morning I wandered into the den a few years ago. I saw the words *Big Apple Bank* at the top of her screen and the word *deposit* over and over down the side of a screenful of transactions. Mom saw me, flinched hard, and shifted the screen—oh so casual—so I couldn't see anymore. It was the best confirmation of what I'd suspected. Mom was getting help for the extras she always came up with that I knew we couldn't afford on her nurse's salary. I'd even heard her on the phone once, before my birthday, asking for "a bit more help for Clae this year."

On the sketchbook page, under the laptop, I write those words: *"A bit more help for Clae."*

Saving the best for last, I turn the page. Here I draw a picture of an oversize brown box I found behind the shoe rack in Mom's closet. A brown cardboard box with a return address in New York City. I stared at it forever, under the flashlight on my phone: 2200 Flatlands Avenue, Apt. 22, Brooklyn, New York.

When I'd peeled back enough tape to see inside, wrapped-up Christmas presents peeked at me. More proof. *Proof* that the extra help was coming from New York. Proof that I must have a fairy god grandma, or maybe an uncle. At least I had a *fairy god somebody*.

That night, I'd written to the return address and asked them to call or message me. Crickets is what I got. But that was before Uncle Wendell and the ring. And the chance to spend a summer in New York, finding out for myself.

In the scrapbook, under *"A bit more help for Clae,"* I write:

> *Fairy God Somebody*
> *2200 Flatlands Avenue, Apt. 22*
> *Brooklyn, New York*

I consider what else to add to the page, but the doorbell interrupts me. I don't answer Mom's call, let her get the door, and listen as she lets Roxy in and explains that I must be in the bathroom. It's time. I have to tell Mom the check is here, for the full amount they promised. In just a few weeks, I'll be gone.

I slide the ring into one back pocket and fold the letter into the other. Then I put the scrapbook in the shoe bin under my bed, and leave the room. On the narrow staircase, I pass Mom's gallery of photographs: me at every age, interspersed with random shots from Black history, from the famous one of Malcom and Martin, to random people Mom thinks I should know but I barely notice anymore.

The smell of hot peaches and baking crust gets stronger with every step, making my mouth water. But as I get to the bottom of the stairs, it's *too* hot, too much, and all I want to do is grab the front doorknob and throw myself into fresh air. There's a not-even-subtle metaphor in there, but I ignore it and, standing in the downstairs hallway, zero in on Mom at the head of the table in our open dining room. She's got a knife in one hand, pastry server in the other, fully focused on plating the perfect slice of the golden pie in front of her. I feel better. Mom is, after all, Mom. *Asha Mitchell, perfectionist*, wouldn't have anything less for her daughter than the best journalism program in the country, even if it is out of state. That part of her is always there—I just need it to block out *Asha Mitchell, lonely single mom.*

"That pie, Mrs. Mitchell," Roxy says, from the guest chair. "I mean . . ."

I slide into the seat next to her and thank her for coming. She shrugs, gathering her red hair over her shoulder, showing more of her pink square-jawed face. She doesn't know she's here so I don't have to be alone with Mom tonight, but she wouldn't care. She loves Mom's baking.

"All right, we ready?" Mom asks. Pressing her lips in concentration, she sinks the knife in, lifts out a triangle, and puts it on a black dessert plate, still-bubbling peaches oozing out the sides. She holds her breath as she finishes the plate with a creamy mound of ice cream. I think how different our art is. But as she holds up the plate to examine her work, I see what's missing. I walk straight to her spot, whip the envelope from my pocket, and hold it out to her.

"The cream on top!" I say. Weak. But at least it's done.

With a snap, Mom's eyes catch mine. She puts down the plate, reaching for the envelope.

"The check? It really came?" She takes it. Shock widens her eyes, and a lot of blinking happens.

I swallow as Roxy looks from one of us to the other.

"There's a list of all the kids that got in, too," I say. "With write-ups about us."

I sound like a little kid, but I can't help it. Now that it's done, I want her to be in her pride, without the hard part. I got a full scholarship to the best summer journalism program in the country. Can it not be about my leaving her?

Her eyebrows sink into their creases as she reads, the black edges of her pinned-up hair pulling against her warm brown skin. Finally, she looks up. "They say a lot of nice things about you," she says. "Your grades, your extras, your application. They're really excited you won that contest."

In the second it takes for her to close the space between us, sadness takes over her face. But then she's hugging me, smelling of butter and hospital cleaner. She pulls away, gives my shoulder a pat, and disappears into the kitchen.

I slump back in my seat, relief slowing my racing heartbeat. There'll be more drama, probably, before I go, but at least I got through that part. Roxy air-elbows me.

"Only you," she says. "Getting *paid* to go to New York."

She grabs the pie, and I nod that she should go for it and keep serving. When we've both got plates, she checks the kitchen, where we can see Mom on her phone.

Roxy drops her voice and says, "You'll finally get to see your dad's family, huh?"

I glare at her. "*Rox!* Not now . . ."

"Well, it's exciting," she whispers, savoring a forkful of pie.

I turn away from her.

Through the window, I can just see the cove behind our house, a strip of silver under the dark blue sky. It's my favorite spot in Gloucester and just looking at it helps clear my head.

I never should have told Roxy about my fairy god somebody. It's complicated. And I only told her part of the story, because it's hard talking to my white friend about my weird Black family, where my mom won't even speak the name of my deadbeat dad. Mom has her little joke she tells me if I try to ask questions: *You know how stereotypes have one grain of truth? Well, that's ours: your father walked out on us—last known address Antigua—and never looked back. So, we don't have to worry about any other Black-folks stereotypes from now on. And we definitely don't have to talk about it.*

But I do worry. *What if my dad did something worse than leave his girlfriend and child? Is he dead? Or in prison? Is he some kind of serious criminal on the run, and that's why Mom won't tell me anything?* I need to find out even though nobody answered my letter. And I'm not explaining all that to Roxy.

"It's not a thing anymore," I whisper, with an edge in my voice. "At least for now. They won't be there this summer."

I ignore how the lie—well, *maybe lie*, since I have no idea what I might find in New York this summer—makes my stomach squirm. Roxy studies me a minute and moves on. "Can I see what the program sent?"

I nod and she picks up the letter from where Mom left it. As she reads, the look on her face is jealous and impressed and a little irritated that I was salty with her. Just real, which is Roxy's best thing and why I like her so much.

She moans and tosses the letter back down. "I should have tried harder in that dumbass essay contest," she says. "I don't want to sell fifty-dollar travel mugs to tourists all summer."

"Do they really pay that much?" Mom asks, coming back in and pulling the pie to her. "Maybe I'll rent this place out and join Clae in New York for a week or so."

We both know she can't take the time off work, but the fact that she's playing with me feels good. Maybe she realizes I really need this summer away, without her.

"Anyway"—she holds up her phone—"I just told Mrs. Brisbaine it's a definite go. You're set to stay with her this summer. Just don't forget, you'll abide by her rules or be on the first bus home."

Right. Everything about this Mrs. Brisbaine—her name; the fact that Mom met her through the most boring nurse at her job, who knew her from some old-people church—irritates me. Like Mom literally found the least fun person in New York for me to stay with.

"So here for it," I say. "I mean, the whole point is to spend time with Mrs. Brisbaine . . ."

"Don't play like her rules are some joke," Mom says, but I get a smile.

Nobody talks as we eat our pie. After Mom polishes hers off, she says she'll do the dishes—probably so she can be alone some more.

I grab the letter and read the best parts again. Picture myself in New York City, on a street full of tall glassy buildings and outdoor cafés, wearing perfect jeans, a cropped tee, and a badass jacket. Everything is so good for future me, I'm not even thinking about how good it is.

Soon. Soon.

It's 2:47 a.m. when I open my bedroom door and slip downstairs to double down on future me's perfect life. I hesitate at the front door, then head to the basement instead. There's no chance Mom'll hear me open the outside door that's down there. Under the light of the bare, hanging bulb, I check the note that took me all night to write.

> *Dear Helper,*
> *I know I've written before, but this time is different. I am coming to New York for the summer. It would mean everything if I could meet you. Please contact me at the number below.*

Short and sweet, and the best I can do. I put it back in the envelope, check the address—2200 Flatlands Ave., Apt. 22, Brooklyn—and lick the seal, before heading out the basement door.

The wind cuts through me as I move into the night. The streetlights are on, but but no lit windows or headlights warm things up. And there're no sounds, besides wind on leaves. *It's going to be fine,* I tell myself, hurrying to the mailbox and sliding my letter in. In the stories, the girl always gets to meet her fairy god person, right? And it's always great when she does.

TWO

CAREFUL WHAT YOU ASK FOR

"Stop it!" I snap, as Mom accidentally stabs me with a plastic hanger. She's that close on my heels as we head into the thrift shop dressing room. One week before I leave, I don't have slack for people running into me. Or making me try on clothes I don't want to wear.

"No, baby, you stop it!" Mom counters, hanging up the clothes and leaning on the wall of the tiny room. "You need some new things for the trip, and these are going to be perfect. You know how we do, you and me."

But I don't know, not this time. Mom and I are unbeatable at thrifting for clothes that look good in Gloucester. But thrifting for clothes that will look right in New York City? Probably impossible in a New England fishing town where most people's idea of fashion involves worsted wool.

Still, I strip down to my underwear, black and decent for trying on clothes. All I want to do is stare in the mirror, which I do all the time since I got the news about New York. What will I look like there, with my glowy dark skin, thick brows, and loose two-strand twists? And my curvy bottom half, so different from most of the girls here. I blink at myself. Roxy says my wide-set catty eyes are *piercing* when I'm not wearing my glasses, which is most of the time. But what if I just look like a deer in the headlights in New York? Or maybe I'll be the same as a thousand other girls—except in a backwoods kind of way.

Avoiding Mom's eyes in the mirror, I pull on the first dress, a straight yellow one that's short and silky and should look good with my skin. It does, but the neck's loose from whoever had it last.

Mom opens her bag and pulls out her little case full of safety pins. Pulling the fabric with a quick tug, she works her strong nurse's fingers and gets the safety pin in just the right spot. The collar lies flat and smooth. Mom grips my shoulders and grins at me in the mirror.

"I still don't want it," I say. And then I'm even more sure I don't want anything we brought in here. "I'm just gonna look online some more. Really."

I've already got my jeans and tee back on, and I'm gathering up the clothes to put on the rack outside the dressing room.

"You've only got a week," Mom says, taking the yellow dress out of my hands. "This is too good a bargain to pass up when it looks that nice on you. I saw some earrings up at the counter, too. They're more than we usually pay, but . . ."

14

I finally look at her. She's got on her weekend outfit: jeans, loafers, button-down with rolled-up sleeves. Her face is full of concern, and I know she just wants to help me get ready for New York. But she can't help with what I need most—to hear back from the fairy god somebody. And so far . . . *crickets*.

"I'm all right," I tell her. "Can we just go?"

She heads to the counter with the yellow dress, and I take one last look in the mirror. When we walk out into the afternoon sun, we head, on autopilot, for the Italian café on the corner where the smell of espresso and anise surrounds us. Since it isn't tourist season yet, the line's quick and we get our favorite seats by the window. Mom takes a sip and literally slips into her sweet spot, eyes closed, lips turned up.

I'm too restless to just sit and sip. When I looked up 2200 Flatlands on Google Earth, it showed a mass of identical tall brick buildings with winding pathways between them. I picture tiny me in a dumb yellow dress in giant New York City. Knocking on a door of somebody who won't even respond to my letters. It's such a crap feeling that I decide to push my luck with Mom.

"What do we know about where I'll be staying in New York?" I ask. "Brooklyn's huge, isn't it? Does Mrs. Brisbaine live, like, downtown?"

"Not even close," Mom says, opening her eyes. "She lives in a quieter part called Sunset Park. Residential, you'll like it."

I look at the menu board posted behind the counter as I ask the next question. "Is it near where you lived when you were there?"

Mom stays calm. "No, but New York's changed since then.

There's nothing I'd recognize, anyway. I know that just from reading the paper."

"You read New York papers?" I ask, surprised.

"You know real estate's my hobby. I keep an eye on New York prices so I always remember how much better they are here. Now, can we talk about something else?" She raises her brows and bugs out her eyes in warning.

I pretend not to notice. "You know we'll get weekends off, right? I think it'd be cool to see where you used to live."

She sighs. "I used to live near downtown. Used to be a lot of Black people down there, and now it's nothing but condos and six-dollar coffee. I told you, I had a good time there, until I didn't. And now, the past's the past." She adds pursed lips to the *warning* look.

I'm not supposed to ask about anything vaguely dad adjacent, even after sixteen years. I'm supposed to know that it breaks her heart, and I'm supposed to leave it alone. Before I can think of how to get around it, Mom talks again.

"You're getting nervous," she says. A statement, not a question. "About going."

I catch her eye and nod.

"Must be strange," she says. "Thinking of being a small fish in a big pond after growing up here."

"How'd you know I felt like that?" I ask.

Mom rolls her eyes. "I know a few things," she says. But I can see she's not really playing. I try holding her eyes, but she looks away. I sip my drink and think about what she said. Big ponds and

16

small fish. When Mom was young, she did the opposite of what I'm doing. Went from a huge city to a tiny town. I make my voice soft and ask another question.

"How was it for you? I mean, moving from the giant ocean of New York to boring little Gloucester?"

"It's not the same at all, Clae," she says. "I had a child to raise, and that's mission impossible in New York for a single mother. At least for me. And you're only going for the summer, not forever. Now let's go." She grabs her purse from the back of her chair.

I'm focused on her now, not just what she can tell me about the past. "Wait," I say. "Did you get what you wanted, moving here? I mean, what if we'd stayed in New York?"

"I have a good kid and a good job," she snaps. "I don't need what-ifs." Her eyes go hollow and I know I've gone too far.

"Mom . . ."

No answer. We're in it now. The ugly place we get to when we talk about the past, especially in ways that remind her of my dad.

I take a sip of my drink. I've always known Mom came to Gloucester for me, because it's cheaper to live and raise a kid. And it seems like being here's why she doesn't have friends outside work. Or boyfriends, for as long as I can remember. But now I'm thinking about the real estate thing. Mom treats her "hobby" like more of a sad obsession—always looking up prices, going to see houses in Boston that she knows she can't afford. Is that why she's doing it? 'Cause she wants to get out of this place she came to for me?

I feel like über-crap for going behind her back to find out stuff about my dad.

"Oh, good!" Mom says. I look up and a big smile's taken over her face. She's got an arm in the air. "Marley, sweetheart! Over here!"

I groan. Marley Evans is in line at the counter, probably pretending not to see us. Because the one thing Marley and I have in common *other* than being the only two Black girls in our grade—or the two grades on either side of us—is wishing our mothers would quit trying to make us be friends.

"Mom . . . ," I start.

But she shouts again, and Marley turns around.

"Nice to see you!" Mom says. "Come chat while you wait for your order."

Marley gives a stiff nod and turns back toward the counter. She's got round shoulders and long skinny arms, and she's wearing a shapeless sundress, with her über-straightened hair in a low ponytail. Exactly the kind of thing that irritates me about her. If we're going to be the only ones, can't we at least put in some effort at style?

"Behave," Mom says, as she pulls an extra chair to our table.

And then Marley's making her way over. She sits, rigid-backed, on the edge of the chair, ready to make a run for it as soon as they call her name.

"Tell us about your summer plans," Mom says.

"Just working," Marley says. "At my dad's office."

"And taking some courses?" Mom prompts.

"Just . . ." Marley's eyes slide over to mine. "Pizza-making class at Stromboli's. And . . . I might join a summer chorus. . . ."

"Must be nice," I mutter, hearing the sarcasm and not caring.

18

Argh. A summer job at her dad's office. No worries about college because her mom works at UMass, so she gets to go for free. Even the pizza thing. One of her ten million aunts works at Stromboli's. Could I try to contain the jealousy that burns under my skin because Marley Evans has the best Black family since the Obamas? Maybe, except she's been rubbing it in my face our whole lives.

"We can't all go to *New York* and get *famous*," Marley says, reminding me that I may have done some rubbing it in, too.

"You're both lucky girls, aren't you?" Mom says, shutting us down. "Now, Marley, your mom says you're trying to top that sweet sixteen of yours with this year's party. Give us a sneak peek! It's only fair, since Clae'll have to come all the way back from New York for it." She throws me the look she and Marley's mom have both got on facial speed dial: *The only two in the whole school? You* will *get along*.

I swallow back the words on my tongue.

"The theme's a secret," Marley says. "But . . ." She chances another look at me. "Even you might like it, Clae. It's gonna be a ton of fun."

"Mmm," I say.

It's another thing with Marley, how she's dull as dishwater 364 days a year, then literally throws the party of the summer every August. It's torture. Her aunts, uncles, and cousins come to town from all over, and I get to watch Marley be the princess of the whole adoring clan.

"Marley!" the barista shouts.

Marley jumps up, and I notice that her earrings are food—a burger in one ear and fries in the other. "Me!" she says. "That's me!"

"Tell everyone hello!" Mom calls as Marley heads to the counter.

There are four drinks waiting for her in a cardboard holder, and I wonder who all she's meeting, but I don't see anyone as she goes out. At our table, Mom falls back into her mad/sad stupor. I shake my head. I am so ready to leave my stupid life in Gloucester.

But before I can dive into a future-me dream, something catches my eye. A wave through the window, behind Mom. When I look up, Zach Teixeira is standing outside the glass storefront. His shiny black curls frame his cinnamon-brown face, and his soft dark eyes kind of beam through his glasses. Seeing him, I suddenly understand who Marley was meeting. He types something in his phone and nods for me to read it.

Zach: When were you gonna tell me? Or was I just supposed to text you one day and you'd be in New York?

Me: We've been over this.

Which we have. I refuse to label the thing that goes on between Zach and me. Or tell anybody about it. I know he thinks I'm playing hard to get . . . which I am. But I have other reasons, too—not the least, that Zach Teixeira is Marley Evans's cousin.

Zach: I don't have to be your boyfriend to deserve some respect.

Zach, Zach, Zach, I think.

Me: Zach, Zach, Zach.

But I'm smiling as I glance back at him, because it's not *such* a bad thing that he's sad I'll be gone for a while. He catches my grin and doesn't seem upset anymore.

Zach: Come out with me later.

For the first time, I think about the fact that I'll miss him, too.

I'll miss a lot of things, I guess. My cove, the beach, Roxy. Mom . . .
even if I need a little space from her, just now.

Zach: I'll get us a boat out and we can hang on the water. I'll bring
the popcorn.

I can almost feel his smile through the window. He knows he
nailed it because it's a great day to be out on the water. And I love
popcorn.

We make a plan. I wait a few minutes, then tell Mom I'm meeting Roxy to hang out on the beach. If she noticed Zach, she doesn't
say anything. And I take off, even though Zach won't meet me for
a while.

It feels good to be outside again. This time of year, downtown
Gloucester's all dressed up and ready for the tourists, the streets
clean, the store windows shiny. I'm so ready to be at the water, I
barely feel the glances that flit my way for too long, like they always
do when I'm alone in town, or just with Mom. I can already feel the
breeze from the ocean. I walk straight into it, knowing that in a few
blocks the world will open into sea and sky. And I'll be alone with
Zach, which, if I'm not lying, feels almost as good.

The beach is wide, rocky, breezy, and beautiful. I walk to where
the waves almost touch, ball my sweatshirt into a pillow, and lay
back on the sand. Finally, my thoughts break free. I picture New
York again, and me in it, and the questions swirl like a summer
storm. *Will it be okay? Will I be enough?* Mom's face breaks into the
scene, sad and mad, reminding me how I messed up at the café.
It'll be nice not to worry about her when I'm in New York—except
I'll probably worry about how much she'd hate it if she ever found

out what I was up to. I rub my gooseflesh arms and look out on the water. Zach's a few yards down the beach, talking to his boat-guy friend.

He's complicated, too.

Even if he weren't Marley's cousin, there'd still be something . . . too obvious . . . about us being together the way he wants us to be. He's chill and easy to be with, and one of the few Black boys for miles. It's like I'm *supposed* to be with Zach. We'd fit perfectly. It's just . . . what if *not* fitting is how I fit in, around here? And Zach makes it so that doesn't work anymore.

I squirm in the cold sand as Zach walks up and holds out a warm hand to pull me to my feet. In no time, he's got us out to the inlet, where we can cut the engine on our little boat and drift. I make myself forget all the weird thoughts. I can just be with him now, today. We rearrange so I'm leaning against his chest under the blanket, and he puts his arms around me. The sun's beginning to set, turning the water to sparkling silver. There's not another boat in sight.

"So are you really such a badass?" Zach asks. "Or are you a little bit nervous about going to New York all by yourself?"

Maybe because I'm looking at the ocean instead of him, it's not hard to tell the truth.

"I'm nervous," I say. "That program's everything. If I nail it, and get a recommendation, it'll way up my chances of getting into good schools, and scholarships, too. But it's really hard."

"Aren't you a straight-A type?"

"Marley told you that?"

"Ha!" he says. "*You* told me that. Remember at Christmas break you said your friend was helping you do an extra-credit science thing so you didn't wreck your average even though you'd bombed a test?"

"Right, yeah . . ."

"So maybe you don't need to worry about grades."

"What?" I actually turn around to face him. "Worry's how come I got Roxy to do the extra-credit thing with me. And I was right to do it!"

Zach shrugs. I settle down again and feel his heartbeat against my back as the water rocks us.

"And there's other stuff to worry about, too," I say. "There's the city, where God knows what people wear. There's friends. Family stuff . . ." I let the words float away, into the tangerine-and-watermelon sky.

"Did I ever tell you my dad might have family in New York?" I ask, after a beat.

"Nah," he says. "Who's there?"

"I'm not sure," I say. "But I plan to find out." I feel lighter having told him, and it's enough for now. He's still warm, still there. "And friends!" I repeat. "What if I can't make friends?"

Zach reaches into the box beside him and pulls out the popcorn.

"You know, you're the first friend I ever made outside my school?" he says. "I was a pretty shy little kid, but you were easy to make friends with."

He pulls open the bag and feeds me a bite, which is good, because I'm not sure what to say. It's a really nice compliment.

We eat popcorn and drink rosé spritzers—compliments of his beach-concession buddies. After a while I pretend to be asleep, just because it's so nice and I don't want to ruin it. And then I get on myself about all the pretending, and I realize maybe I'm not. It's not like I *said* I was sleeping. I just relaxed and shut up, and so did he.

On the way back, he tells me stories about his tennis team and how the coach looks like a Muppet. "Bert without the unibrow, and with Ernie's hair," he says.

"So, cone head or round?" I ask, dredging up my *Sesame Street* memories.

Zach laughs. "You're gonna think I'm lying, but it's kind of triangle shaped, like Kermit's. Funny thing is, the guy's not even bad-looking."

The date's amazing. But I'm leaving for the summer. If there was ever a time to *not* get sappy about Zach, it's now.

THREE

THE OTHER BLACK GIRLS

Dear Clae and Nze,

I'm Joelle. Nice to meetcha! I looked through all our materials and so far we're the Black girl contingent for our track (not everybody has uploaded their pictures yet). Not that I have anything against our non-Black sisters and brothers, just wanted to start bonding! Tell me about yourselves! What made you pick our track? We Black girls gotta stick together, right?

Dear Joelle and Clae,

I'm Nze LaSalle, it's nice to meet you both. I really don't know much about the program. I apply to lots of things and I never know where I'll get in. We'll see, huh? Looking forward to making magic and mischief with y'all. Since I'm from the city, I can show you around.

Dear Clae and Nze,

Clae, are you getting these messages? I'm going to check the list again and write to admin to make sure we have the right address.

I'm sitting with Roxy, feet to feet, on her leather living room couch, both of us on our phones as our food coma wears off from the Chinese takeout feast we just finished. Cartons and napkins and half-full plates cover the coffee table, but the room still feels neat, the fireplace stacked and ready even though it's June, her mom's expensive knickknacks on little tables, reminding me to watch myself. It's nice that her parents and little sister are out, though. We have the place to ourselves on my last afternoon in Gloucester.

I scroll through the three messages again, then open the email from the program to look at the photos they sent. Joelle has a hand on her cheek, like a model shot, and her nails match her royal-blue shirt. Nze is looking up at the camera, teasing it. They're both confident. *Self-possessed*, Mom would say. All the things I work my ass off to be, and that get thin and weak, like paint in water, when I think about New York.

"Don't be, like . . . *coy*," Roxy says.

When I don't get it, she adds, "The program. You must be getting information on what you'll get to do and everything. Is that what you're reading right now?"

I stare at her while my brain refocuses. She's giving me a simple *Just tell me* look. I know I should. But . . . how do you tell your best friend you really, really, *really* want these new friends. Black-girl

26

friends, which she can never be.

To buy time, I look down at my phone. And it dings. Zach's sent a selfie from Marley's backyard, where they're having a family thing. In the pic, he's sitting in a tree. Marley's in the background. And she's staring right at me, like the ghost of frenemies past, warning me to quit bullshitting with Roxy.

I rub my neck. It's not fun being at odds with the only other Black girl around. My mind jumps straight to where it all started. Her *kindergarten* Christmas party. I can still feel how proud I was when Marley's aunt May made a big deal about my new dress. Then Marley whispered in my ear that I couldn't be in their Christmas pictures anyway, because I wasn't family. I already hated her stupid party, with all her aunts and uncles treating her like a princess. But that sealed the deal. And it only got worse with more parties, more years, more ways to irritate each other.

I turn my phone over and focus back on Roxy.

"I got some emails from the school," I say. "There's gonna be a welcome barbecue in some park. And . . . I got emails from a couple girls in the program."

"Well?" Her green-brown eyes hold on to mine. "Do they seem nice?"

"I think so," I say. "We've really just said hi." Even though I'm nervous, it feels good to tell her. But do I say that they're reaching out on the Black-girl channel?

"So far, I've just heard from these . . . these couple of Black girls," I say.

"Oh, okay," Roxy says. There's a pause, then she kicks my foot.

"For Chrissakes, was that so bad, telling me?"

I smile, because I love when she says *fu' Chrissakes* with her full Boston accent. A second later, we both go back to our phones. I think a while, then write.

> Dear Joelle and Nze,
>
> Sorry it took me so long to write back. I'm Clae (pronounced "Clay"). It's really good to meet you. You asked what I'm into. The easy answers are sketching, people watching, and sometimes writing. But here's a more real answer. I had a fortune cookie tonight, and it said, "If you want to find yourself, play hide-and-seek alone." I feel like that's what I do these days. I play hide-and-seek by myself. Looking forward to seeing u soon.

Probably, they'll think I'm a psycho. But I need to be real with *somebody.* So I close my eyes and press send.

Right away, *ping, ping, ping,* three responses come from Nze.

> Loving this! Are you saying you're in the closet and you don't even know it?

> Or, is it like you're hiding from something, and because you're hiding, you can't also seek?

> Or, oh! Maybe you're searching all over the place and you keep on forgetting to look in the mirror?

I am open-mouthed grinning at this when Joelle chimes in:

> Playing hide-and-seek by yourself is about searching for deeper meaning, right, Clae? No one else really knows what you're looking for, so you have to play alone. I think that's so deep.

I haven't figured out what to write back, but Nze and Joelle are already responding, their messages arriving on top of the other. I read Nze's first:

> If we're getting deep, here's my deal. The $ I got for the program didn't include housing, so I'll be juggling that—you know, night to night. Not that big a thing. And I'm not asking for help. But since we're being real, it's good to be.

Whoa. Nze said she was from New York, I remember. So if she lives there, why would she need housing? Does that mean she's *homeless*?

I skip down to Joelle's message:

> I want to tell something real too. Ok, here it is. I'm getting married. Really soon. Except, my parents don't know. Maybe you girls will help me plan!

Even though it's just writing, there's a definite awkward pause. The next message is from Nze:

So . . . congrats! Let's meet at the bbq.

I type:

Congrats! C u in NYC.

Falling back against the couch, all I can think is, *Damn, friend-ships are hard. And I really don't want to screw these ones up.*

FOUR

NEW YORK

I smell car exhaust, sweat, and something deep-fried. There are street vendors and homeless people and stores and restaurants and someone selling designer bags that are spread out on a blanket. The crowd from the bus station melts into the one on the street, the people so much more real than they seemed from the bus windows. I move with a new flow of bodies, across the street and onto the next block, car horns adding to the voices and the music from car windows. Everyone seems separate and different and themselves.

Another block and the crowd thins. I roll my suitcase to a stop beside a line of food carts, just to take a breath. Something sweet and delicious wiggles up my nose.

"You want?" a guy asks. He's selling hot honey peanuts. I buy a bag, realizing that I never touched the lunch Mom packed me. The nuts are warm and crunchy and delicious. There's a breeze and the sun is out, and I bet not one of the people passing me would give a shit if I stood here forever, eating peanuts.

The crossed green signs overhead say that I'm at Forty-Second Street and Ninth Avenue, and Maps tells me the subway to Mrs. Brisbaine's is three blocks away. I buy a second bag of four-dollar peanuts and start walking. I feel too light to even be in my body, but I'm still glad I told Mom and Mrs. Brisbaine the bus was in crazy traffic, and they couldn't predict what time we'd get in. It's better to have a minute to myself.

I mean . . . I'm in New York City. . . .

The subway is huge and bright and dirty. People getting on and off look like models and plumbers and office workers and moms. I read Roxy's texts about her rotten first day of work.

Roxy: The new manager's a nightmare. This guy, Liam. No customers and we still can't take breaks, for Chrissakes.

I send her sad emojis as I get off in Mrs. Brisbaine's neighborhood. It's way quieter than where I got on. So far, nothing I've seen looks like 2200 Flatlands Avenue, and I'm glad. It lets me know that all kinds of places belong in this city.

The streets near Mrs. Brisbaine's are lined with two-story brick houses. I walk up to the right-numbered door feeling at least as tired as I am nervous. Mrs. Brisbaine opens it before I ring.

"All right, good you made it. Now, just to be clear, your mother said you wouldn't be trouble."

"Sorry?" I say.

She picks up the loose gray braid lying across her shoulder and plays with the ends while she looks me over. I look her over, too.

Her skin's the faded beige color of the curtains that hang in our basement, and her brown eyes are faded, too, under pointy grayish eyebrows. The whole thing makes her look *vague, but kind of pissy*. She's wearing what I guess you'd call a housedress.

"Come on," she says. "I'll show you the place." She moves ahead of me, without looking back. "We're going to be timely with each other, you understand? I'm a church referral. People count on me keeping an eye out if someone's young like you. I've been making promises to your momma every day for the last couple weeks."

This whole time, we're walking and just that quick we've covered the apartment. The front door leads to the kind of living room that doesn't look lived in, then we turn right and get to a sunroom. From the couch pillows that pretty much hold her exact shape, I'm guessing Mrs. Brisbaine spends most of her time in there. On the other side of the living room is the hall that leads to the kitchen, a little nook outside it with a table, and the two bedrooms. The whole place smells like cold cuts and the chest-rub stuff for when you're sick.

"All right, then," Mrs. Brisbaine says, head nodding to what must be my bedroom and heading back toward her TV room. "I'll let you get settled. . . ."

I step into my new room and, right off, see two perfect things. Opposite the door is a big window. Through it, there's a row of houses with concrete yards and black iron gates, and they're so *not Gloucester*, they make me feel free as hell. And then there's the lock on the bedroom door. I don't care that the place smells like VapoRub and bologna. Or even that my bedroom walls are a

33

used-to-be-bright yellow that's now like a week-old banana. What-ever. This room's all mine.

It has a twin bed in the back corner with a nightstand next to it, an old wooden desk in front of the window, and a matching dresser next to that. On the wall with the door, there's a closet. I sit at the desk, and my heart races as I look out the window. There're people on the street playing music without headphones, and there's trash on the sidewalk that nobody seems to notice. I remember the feeling of standing on the street, eating peanuts, and nobody giving a damn, but not feeling the least bit lonely, either. I already love this city.

Mrs. Brisbaine's in her nest of pillows when I go back out. Her TV room is the best one in the house, with windows on three sides and a dark blue couch that looks less ancient than the rest of the furniture. Careful not to sound like I'm asking permission, I let her know I'm going out to look around the neighborhood.

"I made cold supper for tonight," she says, still watching the screen. "You can help yourself. Just don't forget the curfew your mother set."

"Right," I say. "Perfect." She nods and turns back to the TV.

Outside, there's a corner store, and, in the middle of the next block, a pizza place. I order two slices, sit in a red plastic chair, and eat with my eyes closed. It's that good. I wonder if I'll ever eat Mrs. Brisbaine's suppers, cold or otherwise. When I open my eyes to take another bite, there's a text from Zach.

Zach: How is it? Also, still thinking about our boat ride.

I smile as I read it. Because I've done some good pillow-snug-gling to the memory of that boat ride.

34

Me: New York's good. The boat was . . .

I add a thinking emoji.

He writes back as I finish my first slice.

Zach: We both know what we both know.

Whatever. All *I* know is . . . my new life is about to start.

FIVE

2200 FLATLANDS

"In point two miles, turn left," Maps tells me when I come out of the subway. It's truth time. Eight in the morning and I don't have to be at the welcome barbecue till twelve. I have the entire morning, and I am 0.2 miles from 2200 Flatlands Avenue—and the possible fairy god somebody.

The blocks by the subway are the kind where the houses and stores are attached to each other, like they're all part of one long building. There are all types of people on the streets, most of them Black. Kids my age hanging out at a café, parents with strollers, guys who look like they're heading for a basketball court. Quick smiles dance across people's faces when they catch my eye. I feel . . . *seen*, but not especially *noticed*. The exact opposite of how I feel in Gloucester.

All this time, I'm walking slow, taking it in. At the corner, I stop to give myself the pep talk. It doesn't matter that my fairy god some-body never responded to my letter. This is a big city. For all I know, they never even got it. Nodding, as if I'm agreeing with myself, I turn the corner. And there they are. The brown brick buildings, set back behind tall iron gates. It's different than it looked online, but I know it's the same buildings. I walk to the entrance, dry-mouthed.

"You going in?" someone asks, and I jump as if he bit me. It's a Black guy, maybe Latinx, in jeans and Nikes. I realize I'm blocking the gate.

"No, sorry." I move out of the way. He takes out a key and opens the iron gate. I try to get a question in my head, but it's hard to know what to ask.

"Apartment twenty-two," I say. "Which building has apartment twenty-two?"

"No idea," he says. "My building's in the hundreds." He locks the gate behind him and disappears.

A few random people go in and out of the complex. On a grassy plot between buildings, I can see people are taking what looks like a tai chi lesson. I look up at all the windows, opened or closed, with curtains or AC units or window boxes. Hundreds of people must live here, maybe thousands. How am I supposed to find who I'm looking for when I don't even know who they are?

I pace the sidewalk. At the corner, a guy pushing a wheelchair stops dead to keep me from walking into the chair.

"Sorry!" I say. Again.

"Watch your step, girl," the guy says, "before you mow us old folks down."

"I will," I say, feeling clumsy. But the old lady in the chair tells me not to mind her bigmouth son. They move on. It was just a quick conversation, but I'm feeling a whole lot about it. A Black man in his fifties or something, and an old woman in a wheel-chair. They're not what I'd pictured, but they could be. I mean, why couldn't they be my uncle and grandma . . . ?

The man pulls out a key and pushes his mom through the gate.

"Hey!" The word comes out too quiet. *"Hey!"*

They're already inside the gate, but the man turns.

"Do you live here?" I ask. "I mean, because . . . I think I know somebody who does, but I don't, I don't know which building."

"What's their name?"

"Mitchell," I say, and then feel a second of confusion, because that's not right. "I mean, Bryant." My dad's last name slides out easy enough, considering I'm not sure I've ever said it out loud before. Once I say it, it's like I can see it in the air.

"Mitchell Bryant?" the man asks.

"No, not Mitchell. Just Bryant. Richard Bryant."

"Sounds like a clothing label," he says. "But, no. This is a big place, and those are pretty average names. Sorry I can't help."

He waits a second to see if I have any other questions. I wish I did—I've already tried finding Richard Bryant online, and there are too many to count. I don't know what I expected.

"Would . . . could I come in?" I ask. "I just want to watch the tai chi, and maybe my . . . my uncle will start answering his phone and I can find him."

The guy leans down to the woman in the wheelchair. "What do

you think, Ma? Think she's a danger to our community?"

"Let the girl in," the old woman says with a smile.

My voice sounds scratchy when I thank them.

There are benches by the tai chi. Kids are everywhere, tiny ones playing on wooden animals and mini climbing structures, older ones watching them. Lots of senior citizen types sitting on benches, reading or talking. It seems like a nice place to live. And I am crazy nervous, being here.

I mean . . . what exactly am I doing? Best-case scenario, I find a relative and they tell me what went down with my dad. But there's almost no chance that it's good news, or else Mom wouldn't be so dodgy about it. I want to know, yes. I need to know—but now that I'm here, it seems sadder and harder. I can't ask every person here if they're related to me. I reach into my pocket, slip a finger inside the J. M. Smith High ring, which I brought along for luck.

Thinking of my evidence book, I take a picture of the shiny black door the guy and his mom went through. Then, I walk. Instead of being numbered, the buildings are color coded, a thick band of paint at the bottom of each: blue, green, yellow, brown, tells you which is which. I move along the concrete paths that run between them. And then I see a door. Standing open. It's a side door, green metal, probably leading to a basement. If I went in . . . I could maybe get an elevator up to the apartments? See the numbers. Maybe I'd find number 22, or at least see the patterns so I could figure out which building number 22 is in . . .

There are people on the paths, but no one's near the door. I move closer. It's just a couple of inches open. Casually, I look inside.

It's dark. I can only see a plain cement floor and a few fat columns. Nobody's in there.

I slip inside. As my eyes adjust, I see metal storage cages on one end. There are other doors along the walls, all closed, and a place where brooms and mops are piled against a wall. Finally, I spot the elevator—more green metal—on the other side of the room. I could walk around the edges, so I wouldn't be out in the open. But that would take longer. I take a breath and move into the middle of the floor, telling myself it's gonna be worth it. Finding number 22 will change everything.

"Can I help you?"

I freeze.

The male voice gets louder. "Can I help you, sweetheart?"

I turn toward it. He's middle-aged, bald, white. Wearing some kind of work overalls.

"I'm looking for my grandma," I say. "She's . . . lost."

"Okay, sorry, but she's not here. Why don't you go look by the tai chi, the old girls like that."

Not believing my own nerve, I say, "Can I just go upstairs? She likes to ride the elevators."

"That's the utility elevator. You gotta go around."

I nod. He's not that scary, but I still don't like moving past him. His footsteps follow me to the door, and when I step into the sunshine, I'm grateful, like I just escaped a dungeon.

I don't stop at the tai chi but keep going, straight out of the complex. What was I thinking? Me alone in the basement with some random man . . .

For someplace to be, I duck into the café on the corner. It's small, just two tables pushed up against the wall. That could have been bad . . . I have to get a grip.

At the counter, I ask for a latte, give the guy my name, and hand over my cash. As I'm getting my change, a voice behind me says, "Did you say Clay? What kind of name is that for a nice-looking girl?"

The voice is deep, definitely coming from a Black guy. I turn around to see long-enough-to-be-messy hair, a stubbly beard, skin darker than mine, and steady brown eyes that stay put on my face instead of flitting around like a lot of guys' do.

"It's just my name," I say. "Nickname. Short for McCauley."

"Interesting all around," he says, still grinning.

"Hate to interrupt, but can I get your order?" The man behind the counter doesn't hide his sarcasm.

The guy kind of blushes. "Can I get a coffee, black and sweet?" He glances at me.

I don't get the joke till the counter guy says, "Niiiice," then stage-whispers, "you can slip me a note if that's not what you really want."

They both laugh. Since I don't know what to say, I move to the wait-for-your-order end of the counter. The guy's still paying, so I get to check him out for a sec. He's got on a purple hoodie and jeans that show off his butt. Then he's heading over to me.

"I'm Clay," he says.

"What?" I'm so surprised, I forget to be nervous. "No way! Your name's Clay?"

But he's already got a hand over his face, trying to cover his embarrassment. He shakes his head, then slowly slides his hand down to uncover one eye.

"Nah," he says. "Nah, that didn't come out right. *You're* Clay. I'm Bolt."

It takes me a minute to digest what a sad move that was, then keep myself from making fun of him. "Okay . . . *Bolt*," I say. "Because you're fast?"

He laughs another embarrassed laugh, shakes his head again. "Because my last name's Bolton," he says.

This time I can't help laughing. Someone behind the counter calls my name, and I turn to get my drink.

"You live around here?" Bolt asks.

"No. My—my grandmother does. At the complex across the street. What about you?"

"I live over there, too! I'm supposed to be meeting some people now, but . . . maybe I can get your . . . ?" He doesn't seem to have the nerve to say "number," but he holds up his phone and wiggles it in his hand. For all his goofiness, saying the wrong name and everything, his eyes still don't leave mine as he waits for an answer. I like that. And the chocolate skin doesn't hurt, either.

"Um . . ." Mom's warnings about strange men kick in and I stop.

"All right, well. You visit your grandma a lot?" he asks.

"My . . . ?"

"Your grandma. Maybe I can see you next time you come."

"Right." I can't believe all the fake relatives I keep coming up with, but I go with it. "She likes the tai chi, you know, out in the yard. Maybe I'll see you around there. . . ."

Someone calls his name then, and he turns to get his coffee.

"So," he says, drink in hand, pointing a finger at me. "Next time."

After he takes off, I grab an empty seat and let the smile spread across my face. My first New York flirting, and with a guy from 2200 Flatlands Ave. After a minute, it hits me that I really might see him again, next time I come to snoop around. I get my mind off his pretty eyes and pull up the Notes app on my phone.

Questions for Bolt next time:

Which building has number 22?

Has he ever heard of the J. M. Smith High School?

Is there a way to talk to his mom or grandma?

How can I get inside a building—does everybody have keys? Do people let each other in?

When I'm done, I look around the little café, the street outside the plate glass window. I like it here. But what happened in the basement reminds me that I don't belong. Not really. Not yet.

SIX

SLEUTH IN THE CITY

My head's still at 2200 Flatlands as I take the subway, then follow my GPS to Washington Square Park for the welcome barbecue. I'd been so close. *If I'd got in that elevator and found number 22, what could have happened? Would I have had the guts to knock? And who, who, who would have opened the door?*

I cross a street, and there's the park, in front of me. All kinds of people are spread out on the grass and walkways, talking, playing, eating. In a flash, first-day-of-school jitters take over my 2200 Flatlands feelings.

There's music playing. The park has a big stone archway, a reflecting pool, and tables with built-in checkerboards. Fancy and friendly all at once. The second I get to the gate, I spot Joelle. Her hair's short and natural, like in the picture, but with a white baseball cap perched backward on top of it. Her white jumpsuit's offering much cleavage, and she has on green baby-heeled thong sandals. The girl she's talking to looks like she's had enough of her. I duck out of the way. For some reason, I want to meet Nze first.

A quarter way around the park, I spot her with a bunch of people dancing to the live band. I know from the picture that it's her, but she's thicker than I thought, wearing a blue cropped tee that shows a strip of belly over white sweatpants. Her braids are loose and sleek, and she can move. I should jump in, surprise her. It's not like I can't dance. But . . . too soon, I guess.

Not far from the dancers, there's an official-looking table with folders and name tags. So I don't get caught staring like an idiot, I go over.

"Clae Mitchell," I say to the ponytailed white girl behind the *M–Z* sign.

"*Clay?* Sorry, I don't—"

"I mean, McCauley," I say. "Can we change that on things? I go by Clae—*C-l-a-e*."

She looks overwhelmed. "Um . . . what'd you say your name is? The one that would be on here?"

I spell out McCauley and then Mitchell. In my brain, I play with the name Bryant again. Clae Bryant? Who would she even be?

"Gotcha!" The girl smiles, hands me a name tag and a folder, and starts rattling off information. "Food's over by the Garibaldi statue, hot dogs, but there's some plant-based stuff. They'll be gathering us together in a bit for a short welcome. In the meantime, have fun!"

I move away, my eyes finding Nze again. I know homeless

45

people don't look one certain way, but I still think she doesn't look homeless. Or is that just wrong to think? As I'm looping this in my head, she looks straight at me. Our eyes catch, and she jogs over.

"Clae?" she says. "Hey!" She hugs me like we're old buds. "You made it. Have you seen Joelle yet?"

"Only got signed up," I tell her, showing my new red folder. She leads the way to an empty bench and sits with her toes and knees pointing in, elbows on her thighs. Next to us, old men play chess at a couple of the tables.

"I like this park," I say.

"Might be my favorite," Nze says. She smiles with her whole face, which is the color of dark honey. She's got big eyes, round cheeks, perfect teeth. I like her right off and figure everybody must.

"So, where do you—" I break off before I say "live," realizing my mistake. My face goes hot, and I close my eyes to not have to see her expression.

"It's all good," Nze says. "I was probably too dramatic with how I told you. Tonight, I'm staying with a friend in Battery Park, not even far from here. All safe and indoors."

I scrunch my face, lips twisted to one side. "Sorry if you didn't get the part where I'm the clueless girl from the New England sticks. . . ."

"No, I got it," she says, flipping her braids and grinning. "Where're *you* staying? In the dorms?"

"I wish," I say, relaxing because she seems over my mistake. I'm about to break out the story of how Mrs. Brisbaine met me at the door complaining, when I hear someone squeal my name.

"Clae? Nze? *Lay-dees,* it's so good to see you!"

Nze and I trade the quickest glance before we get up to hug Joelle. Close-up, she's different than her pictures. She's tall with silky dark skin. There's a sort of imbalance to her—skinny, but with giant boobs—pretty, but with something needy in her clear brown eyes.

"Okayyy!" Nze says. "Nice jumpsuit."

"You're sweet!" Joelle says, as all three of us sit down on the bench.

"Should we go eat?" I ask, because there's a pause and I can't think of anything else to say.

They both shrug, but we get up anyway, and Nze leads the way across the park.

A middle-aged Black guy stops us, holding up a handful of markers and colored pencils. "What's on your heart today?" he says. "Tell it right here. A thought, a poem, a picture."

A bunch of people are on the ground, grouped around a giant sheet of mural paper. Nze squats down to join them. The mural's almost full; there are poems, artwork, and big loopy signatures.

Happy to get a pencil in my hand, I squat, too, and draw 2200 Flatlands Avenue: tall buildings with tons of doors, shiny black and dull green, all over the place.

"Jeezy-wheez, you're good!" Joelle says. She looks over at Nze. "And you, too!"

"I just wrote what I see," Nze says. "All of us, here, meeting for the first time."

I look down at what she's done.

Quick, take the picture
Pride, plans, possibility
Stretched out on the grass

"Wow," I say. "You just thought of that?"

"I like haiku," she says. "It's so much easier than finding words the regular way."

Joelle, who didn't draw or write anything, hands the mural guy some money. We keep going on the path until we hear, "Testing, testing! Can you all hear me?"

It's a Black man, about Mom's age, booming into a microphone by the sign-in table. He's got on teacher casual: joggers, Adidas, one of those textured short-sleeved collar shirts. In a loud, happy voice, he tells us to gather in, he's Mr. Barber, head of the program. The three of us grab seats on an empty bench.

"Welcome to Sleuth in the City!" Mr. Barber shouts. "Be honest. How many people came here for the name? We love that name because if you're a journalist, you're a sleuth! You're a gumshoe, a detective, a bloodhound, a PI. If you're doing it right, you're even a secret agent, because you'll have sources you can't reveal. And you're going to start all that right here!"

The crowd whoops. Joelle and Nze both clap, and I take a minute to look closer at them. Nze's settled into herself, almost like she's alone on the bench. I noticed it about her when we were walking, too. If she's not talking to you, she's in her own world. The thing with Joelle is, she seems older than me and Nze, which helps explain the getting-married thing. She sees me looking, leans across

Nze, and whispers, "Chaz might meet us here, later. Chaz, that's my fiancé."

"Whoa." Nze swivels her head to look at Joelle.

"If I'm in the city, he usually meets me to take me home," Joelle says. "But now that I'm staying in the dorms, he's just gonna come say hi."

Nze sends me a quick *Oughta be interesting* look before turning back to Mr. Barber at the mic.

"What makes a great piece of journalism?" Mr. Barber asks. "Well, we don't call them *stories* for nothing. Great journalism has compelling characters. There's *power* being used or abused. And it tells some hard truths. We live in a time when information is everywhere, but the *truth* is thin on the ground. When you can embed hard facts in a good story? *That's* when people begin to *understand, think, act*. That's the power of good journalism!"

"Wait till you see the swag bags," Joelle whispers, pointing.

While Mr. Barber's been talking, somebody unloaded dozens of white gift bags onto the registration table.

"My mom knows him, Mr. Barber, because she's an alum at the university and she does volunteer stuff. He let me help with them."

"This guy?" I ask, nodding to Mr. Barber. "You already know him?"

Joelle shrugs.

"Which brings us to your first assignment!" Mr. Barber says. "You're each going to pitch me a fantastic story, young friends! You'll hear more about this, but I'm telling you today because you never know when you'll pass a story on the street. One might already be lurking inside your heads and you don't even know it's there! Might be hard news, investigative, an in-depth feature . . ."

He rubs his hands together and yells, "All things are possible! So, minds open and ears up! Now, go on, get some food," he says, pointing to the table. "And get to sniffing!"

People clap, and there's a rush for the swag table.

"Well, that was . . . high energy," Nze says as we take our place in line.

"But what about that assignment?" I ask. "Are we really supposed to just find a story somewhere on the street?" I'm not ready for school stress to start yet.

"I've already got my topic," Joelle says.

"What, you got the jump 'cause you know the director?" Nze asks.

Joelle looks offended. "I read the intro materials like everybody else," she says. "I only offered to help with the swag bags because I thought somebody our age would be better at picking stuff."

"No shade!" Nze says, like she means it.

"No problem," Joelle says, less so.

Tension noted. I've never been great at three-way friendships, and these two are making me nervous. We get our bags at the table. They have Sleuth in the City hats and water bottles, a New York City explorer kit, and discount coupons for restaurants and stores.

"The coupons?" Joelle says. "All Black-owned businesses. How dope is that?" She checks her phone, and says, "Oh, crap. Chaz's gonna be a while. He's helping a homeless guy." She looks at us, beam-smiling. "He really is the sweetest, most adorable guy. You'll see."

"Can't wait," Nze says, avoiding my eyes.

"Maybe I should just meet him halfway," Joelle says. "Y'all want to come with? We've got a favorite spot in Brooklyn, like between the Brooklyn and Manhattan Bridges. We could take food from here and go eat in the park there, and then he could meet us when he's done."

"I'm in!" I say, ready to see more of the city, especially Brooklyn.

And we're off to raid the food tables.

"Wait, this is Brooklyn? " I ask, as we walk into the fanciest park I've ever seen. It overlooks a river with a huge bridge in the distance and signs for roller skating, pickleball, and bouldering, whatever that is. "I thought Manhattan was the big-money part of New York?"

"Nah, Brooklyn's mad gentrified," Nze says. "So we've got all the expensive stuff, too. This park was a dump when I was little. Literally. But there's lots of the old stuff still around, too." What she says makes sense to me. It's how the city feels—like it's full of disguises and surprises, like anything might happen, and probably already has.

Joelle leads the way to a spot on the grass with a view of the bridge. She opens her bag and pulls out the food she took from the barbecue, making a tablecloth from a thick layer of napkins and topping it with water bottles, hot dogs wrapped in foil, and little ice cream cups. Nze and I add the stuff we grabbed—bags of chips and more hot dogs—and it looks like a feast. Joelle messages Chaz where to meet us, and I dig in, because I haven't eaten since this morning.

"Did you know," Joelle says, pointing to the older of the two bridges we can see, "that *I Am Legend* was filmed right over there? They had great monster makeup in that movie, and costumes. That's what I'm thinking of doing for my project—something on film, makeup, and fashion, you know? Maybe just films made in New York."

"We should work together," Nze says. "Do something amazing. Though . . . maybe not movies and makeup."

"I'm up for working together!" I say, loving that I wouldn't have to pitch Mr. Barber a *fantastic story* all on my own.

"I even have some thoughts . . . ," I say. Which is true in the sense that I got an idea of an idea when Mr. Barber was talking.

Joelle throws up a hand to shut me up. "Slow down, sis! It's not even day one. Remember, I've still got a whole wedding to plan."

"All right, yeah," Nze says. "What about that, anyway? Why you getting married so young?"

Joelle sits up on her ankles, suddenly serious. "Why wouldn't I? I met the right person, I want to marry him, and I'm eighteen years old. Why is that anybody else's business?"

"I get that," I say. "It's nobody's business, not even your parents'. You should do what you want."

"When you put it that way," Nze says, "I see you. There's too many things people want to control, huh?"

"You too?" Joelle asks. "Who's doing the controlling in your life . . . or trying to?"

"Who and *what*," Nze says. She looks at us Roxy-style, raw and real, for a long minute.

This time, Joelle and I share a look, waiting. But then Nze shakes her head and shimmies her shoulders, and her bright smile's back in place.

Joelle and I keep staring at her, and she says, "Not today, women. We'll see. Maybe by the end of the summer we'll know all each other's secrets."

All three of us trade looks, smiling a little at the thought. Then Joelle checks her phone and, like a tic, so do I. Mrs. Brisbaine's forwarded a text chain between her and Mom.

Mom: Curfew is the same on Sundays as weekdays, correct?

Mrs. B: 10 pm unless there's a school function or prearranged activity. Correct?

Mom: Correct.

Mrs. B: Correct.

"Did somebody say something about control?" I mutter, before moving on to a text from Roxy with more complaints about her job.

Roxy: So boring. We're supposed to "get to know the merchandise" instead of hang out between customers.

Joelle interrupts with a squeal. "He'll be here in two!" She goes in her bag, pulls out lipstick. "We won't talk wedding planning the whole time," she says. "But Chaz isn't one of those guys who leaves it all on the bride. He's on this journey with me, one hundred percent."

"Is he rich?" Nze asks. "Is that how you're paying for a wedding without your parents?"

Joelle gets a defensive look. "*He's* not rich. He's . . . just . . . resourceful. And anyway, it's all on the cheap. We'll buy my wedding dress, picnic food, and flowers, but no, like, venue. We're doing city hall and then a big, super-perfect picnic in the park across the street."

I have to clamp my lips to keep from letting out a "*wow.*" *I mean, if you're gonna plan a secret wedding, why do it at city hall?*

Nze, of course, asks out loud.

"It's nicer than you'd think," Joelle says. "You get a private room, and you can bring flowers and stuff to zhuzh it up. The plan is, we invite our parents to this fancy restaurant for brunch, and we make a reservation for all of us, but when we get there, they tell us the reservation's for an hour later. So Chaz says, we're right by city hall and he needs to get a passport application, let's go over there to kill time." Joelle's voice gets higher with every line.

"And I just keep talking to my parents so they don't notice the signs are pointing to the marriage part not the passport part, while Chaz leads us straight to our assigned room. We'll have some friends there, and Chaz's parents, who will be all set with the flowers and—"

"Didn't you say you were doing a wedding dress?" Nze interrupts. "Won't that make it kind of obvious?"

"I'm going to say I'm getting over a cold and need to wear a coat . . ."

"Wow." I just go ahead and say it. It's the most elaborate, doomed-seeming plan I've ever heard. About a million things could go wrong!

"Yeah, so—" But this time Joelle cuts herself off with a shriek, as she jumps up and runs across the grass. A few seconds later, she throws herself at a skinny bearded white guy who's walking our way. They stay there a long minute, hugging each other.

"Awwww shit," Nze mumbles. "I didn't see that coming. The man's name is Chaz, but I still didn't see it coming. You?"

"Noooo," I admit.

The way Joelle talks, *Black girls gotta stick together, Black-owned businesses*, it never occurred to me that Chaz was white. The two of them finally break apart and head back across the grass.

"This," Joelle says, squeezing his arm, "is Chaz. Chaz, these are my new girls, Clae and Nze. Sit down, I brought ice cream for you."

Chaz sits cross-legged on the grass. He's got on shorts and a loose black tee, and his brown hair, thick and bushy like his beard, is tied in a ponytail.

"It's always great to meet Joelle's friends," he says. "They've all been exceptional." He grabs an ice cream cup, and since it's mostly melted, takes a drink. "Oh, this is *wonderful.*"

"Isn't it?" Joelle says. "Isn't it amazing?"

I can feel Nze trying not to laugh.

"What happened with the homeless person you were helping?" Joelle asks Chaz.

"Okay, good story," Chaz says, wiping his mouth from the ice cream. "I'm on the LES—Lower East Side—and he's just hanging on the street, up against the wall outside a school. He's got his cup out, so I give him a five. He looks up and says thanks, but I can tell he's not really feeling it, so I ask what's up, if he needs more, or what. And he says the five's good, but then he goes, 'What I really need is some respect.' And he tells me about this place that kicked him out, even though he had money to pay. So we went back. It was this cupcake shop, and there was a brother behind the counter this time. And get this." He gives Joelle puppy dog eyes. "He's the owner, and he's mad about what the other guy—like his employee—did. So, he gives my guy free cupcakes, and the next thing you know he and I are talking wedding, babe. And I think he can do the cupcakes for us, basically for cost, as long as we get 'em to Jersey ourselves."

Joelle squeals again. "See! Can you believe him?"

I can't. Everything about him is intense: the way he talks, like every word is the most important ever, and especially the way he looks at Joelle. Like she might disappear if he takes his eyes off her.

"My mom loves cupcakes," Joelle says. "So it's perfect."

"For the picnic?" Nze asks.

"Exactly! I mean . . . if they stay, my parents." A flash of fear crosses her face before she rolls her eyes and says, "But of course they'll stay."

Something about her expression makes me think about my fairy god somebody—who I'm starting to think of as the FGS—and the letter that never got answered. I guess I'm not the only one into wishful thinking.

"The problem is, the dress," Joelle says. "I've been putting it off because it's the main part my mom would be sad about missing."

"So, we're just gonna do it together, right?" Chaz says. "One more way we're kicking sexist traditions in the face."

There's an awkward pause, because Joelle doesn't answer and doesn't look at Chaz.

"What?" Nze says. "You want us to go shopping with you, so Chaz doesn't have to?"

"I can't ask my friends at home, because I'm scared they'll tell my mom," Joelle says, looking nervous. "And it is kind of . . ."

"A time a girl wants her girls," Nze says. "We got you."

"You do?" Joelle says. "That would be soooooooo amazing!"

It would, I think. If the three of us could have each other all summer long? Amazing it would be. I grab an ice cream cup and cross my fingers as I eat it.

SEVEN

FIRST CONTACT

I dress carefully, like every other first day of school. Based on what I saw at the barbecue, the outfit I picked should work. Good jeans, a short tee with the shoulders cut out, one arm full of bangles. My hair's acting up, but I give myself the scalp-scratching treatment Mom's so good at, and it works. For my final touch, I take Uncle Wendell's ring from the bedside drawer and slip it in my pocket.

When I get to the kitchen, Mrs. Brisbaine's already there. She's got the table covered in eggs, bacon, and these biscuits that look like she stole them off a Food Network set.

"It's my breakfast special," she says, with an actual wink. "It's why the church keeps sending me people. You're not getting this anyplace else in New York City."

"Mrs. B! It's . . ." I grab a biscuit and bite into tender butteriness. "Oh my gosh, so good!"

Mrs. B. watches me chew, so I make deliciousness sounds and smack my lips. By the time I finish, we've definitely had a moment.

When I get off the subway, the GPS leads me through a neighborhood full of white stone buildings and the kind of restaurants that have guys outside just to open the door for you. Unlike the part of the city where I got off the bus, this feels like a place where people give plenty of shits, especially about people who don't belong hanging out in their streets. The last block has taller, glass buildings. I find the revolving door to ours and push through to a high-ceilinged lobby. A sign reads *SLEUTHERS: 27 Studio B.* I catch sight of a kid I saw in the park and follow him onto the elevator, where he presses number 27.

"The twenty-seventh floor?" I blurt out. "I've never been that high up."

He looks unimpressed. When we get there, I let the kid go in front of me and push away thoughts that I'm going to suck at the program and Nze and Joelle are gonna blow me off once they meet everybody else. Another sign points us to Studio B, and I walk the long hallway alone.

Studio B is a carpeted room with rows of desks and a wall of windows. I go straight over. When I look up, the clouds feel close.

"It's nice, right?" Joelle says, joining me from somewhere. She's holding a big cold cup with a metal straw and wearing jeans and a tank that shows off her arms and boobs. She's got on another baseball cap, this one blue to match the top. "Let's sit here, so if it's boring we've got the view," she says. She takes the second seat from the window, puts her bag on the third one, for Nze, and leaves the one closest for me. Something inside me slides into place. It might just be okay.

I take my seat as the room fills around us. Mr. Barber shows up just after Nze, who looks like she's already had a day, considering it's nine in the morning. Mr. Barber greets us too loud and writes on the whiteboard: *Ugly Tweet v. Journalism. Go!*

"Gotta give him a gold star for enthusiasm," Nze says, settling back in her chair.

Mr. Barber starts the class. "Here's what you're thinking," he says. "Guaranteed! You're thinking, 'Who doesn't know how to be a journalist these days?' You find something interesting, you go online and search around, then tweet it out, or BuzzFeed it, or whatever it is you do. Boom! You're a journalist!

"Well, let's see, shall we?" He gives a dramatic pause, then says, "I'm about to use four words you might never have heard in a classroom before. *Take out your phones!*"

We all wait a beat before it sinks in, and then there's a rustle of sound as everybody gets theirs.

"I'm going to ask you to find the best story you can," Mr. Barber says. "The sweetest piece of breaking news you can find from a social media site. Any story posted by regular people or groups—but not trained journalists. You're going to find the headline, read the stories, and then we're gonna analyze what we've got. That's the assignment. You have ten minutes to scroll whatever you like to find the hottest news you can." He picks up his own phone off the desk, looks at the time, and says, "Okay! What are you waiting for?"

"Huh," Nze mutters. "Not bad."

Everybody gets started.

When I look at my phone, there's a text from Zach. It just says, First Day with three fire emojis, but it makes me smile. I mean, it's nice he remembered. I start to write back that I'm in class and can't talk, when another text comes in. I freeze.

It's from an unknown 718 number. I know from Mrs. Brisbaine that 718 is Brooklyn. My face and neck go hot because I feel suddenly sure it's the FGS. So sure, that I'm also sick with worry that it's not. I look over at Nze and Joelle. They're both scrolling on their phones.

I open the message.

Unknown: Why?

Why . . . ?

I type, Why what? But then I realize with a sharp gut pain that I know the answer. The last thing I wrote to the FGS was *I am coming to New York.* And now they want to know why. It's the reason they're writing back after all this time. Because I'm here now and they want to know why I came.

My pulse bashes my eardrums so hard I can't tell what's happening in the rest of the classroom. I take a quick look out the window. Now that I'm sitting, I can't see anything but clouds in the pure blue sky. Somewhere out there, the FGS is waiting for my message.

Me: To see you.

Then I erase it, because that might freak them out. I go online, find a link to Sleuth in the City, and paste it into the message. Then add:

Me: And to see you.

I glance at Nze and Joelle. They're both deep into the assign-ment. I hit send and stare at the phone. An answer comes.

Unknown: And if I tell you there is no great excitement in meeting
me?

Me: I want to, anyway!

Unknown: Ah. Well.

Unknown: There is an African proverb that says, Patience can
cook a stone. I ask you to try it.

Patience? I swallow back a hurtful thickness in my throat.

Me: I've been patient a long time. Can you just tell me who you
are?

Before I hit send, I change it to:

Me: Can you please just tell me who you are?

There's noise in the room now, as I wait for another answer. I realize that time's up on our assignment. People are raising their hands to let Mr. Barber know what they found. I ignore them and stare at my screen, my whole body asking the questions: *What is happening? Is this real? And if it is—how are they asking me to be patient? Am I finally talking to a real person, not just shooting arrows in the dark, and they're still blowing me off?* Then the answer comes:

Unknown: Another proverb says, Courage, Common Sense, and
Insight are precious friends. The proverb does not speak of curi-
osity.

Huh . . . ? As I'm trying to figure it out, Joelle starts talking from the seat next to me. I hear the words *Halloween* and *Cheetos*, and I look over, and she catches my eye, then turns back to Mr. Barber.

"But the story only says that some guy got arrested for having the Cheetos laced with fentanyl," she says. "And that it happened a month before Halloween. There's nothing to say he was actually going to give the stuff to trick-or-treaters. But the headline makes it sound like it happened and all the parents better check their kids' bags."

Mr. Barber looks impressed. But before he says anything, my phone vibrates in my hand.

I literally jump.

Unknown: I'll be in touch.

Me: When?

The word hangs on my screen, and I know, the way you just do, that the conversation's over.

Slowly, the classroom noises come back. "Go on, Leopold," Mr. Barber says, and an Asian boy speaks up about the same Halloween story Joelle talked about. I try to tune in, if only to not think about what just happened.

"I'd have interviewed kids and parents in the area to see if anybody actually got any funky snacks," he says. "It's not enough to have something that *could have* gone out. And anyway"—he looks around for reactions before he even says his next line—"who puts *Cheetos* in Halloween bags?"

He gets his laugh, and Mr. Barber says, "Good point."

I take a few deep breaths, tuning back out. *I'll be in touch . . .*

EIGHT

BELLY BUTTON GUNK

"What was that about?" Nze asks. "You were gone that whole class."

"So we're done?" I ask. But we're the last people in the room, so it's a dumb question. "I mean . . . what's next?"

"Break," Nze says. We have it easy since some of our classes don't start till next week."

She and Joelle lead the way back to the elevators. Before I realize where we're going, we're in a huge cafeteria. Like the classroom, the whole back wall is windows. We join the line to grab food.

"Wherever you were during class, it looked interesting," Nze says when we're at a table, she and I with snacks and drinks on our plain gray trays, Joelle with a brown paper bag she brought with her.

Nze goes on. "Interesting, but it got to you, whatever it was. It freaked you out." She opens her chips, takes the lid off her salad, generally makes herself comfortable for whatever I've got to say.

Joelle does the same, arranging her PB and J and apple on the outside of her bag.

I go out of body for a minute, seeing the scene from outside my own head. Here I am, sitting near a window overlooking New York City, with two Black girls who feel like new friends. I sigh. *Can I really tell them about the FGS when I've never told anybody? And anyway, would it wreck everything if they knew I've never even had Black-girl friends before?*

"I just . . . got a text," I say. "Long story . . ."

"You got someplace to be?" Nze asks.

I suck on half my bottom lip. I'm seriously thinking of telling them what I never told Roxy, which makes me feel a way. But . . . I just need to tell.

"Did you mean it, yesterday?" I ask. "About telling each other secrets? Because this is . . ."

"Of course we meant it!" Nze says. "As long as it's real deal. Not *I pick my belly button gunk when nobody's looking* kinds of secrets."

"Eww," Joelle says. "But yes, real secrets. No navel gunk."

I can't hold it in. I tell them about Uncle Wendell and the ring, the phone conversation I overheard, the box of Christmas presents, even the bank transfers. I end with the letters I sent to 2200 Flatlands Avenue and the field trip I took there before our welcome barbecue. Finally, I hand over my phone and watch them read the FGS's texts.

They take forever. Finally, Joelle looks up, shiny-eyed.

"That must be incredible," she says. "A fairy god person. Like, for real."

"Oh," I say. "I know I call it that, but it's not . . . it's really about the family part."

"That they might be related to your dad?" Nze asks. "Because you never knew him. So getting to have a part of him would be the magic, huh?"

It's so on point that tears prick my eyes. Joelle reaches over and puts her hand on mine. I stay quiet a minute and feel the love. As my breathing calms down, a thought tugs at my mind.

"Do you think they might've seen me when I was there?" I ask. "The FGS. Do you think they saw me when I went snooping at 2200 Flatlands, and that's why they finally decided to contact me? Because they'd obviously know who I am, right, if they've been sending me stuff all this time. So, they *could* know what I look like!" I'm not even sure why I like the idea, but I do. The FGS knew me. Recognized me. And then they reached out.

"You could ask them," Nze says.

I shake my head. I'm already worried they'll never "be in touch" anyway, and asking more questions won't help.

Joelle leans in, looking mischievous. "There are other ways of finding things out," she says. "I can help you figure out stuff about this FGS. You'd just have to come to my dorm room. You wanna come later, after we're done?"

"What do you mean, you could help me figure out stuff to do with the FGS?" I ask.

"You have to see it to believe it," Joelle says, wiggling her brows under the brim of her hat.

"Well, I can't," Nze snaps. "I've got a doctor thing after last class." She pulls out her laptop. "And I have to fill out these stupid forms for them, too. Same forms every *single* new doctor."

"What is it?" I ask, distracted from Joelle because Nze sounds so pissed.

Nze glares at the form, then flips the laptop over for me to see. "They list every disease anybody's ever heard of, and I have to say if I or a family member ever had it." I start to look at the form, but she snatches it back. "You know what?" she says. "Never mind. I'd rather take a turn with this telling-secrets thing we're doing. I mean, if you're done, Clae?"

I nod.

"It's not a secret, exactly," Nze says. "I want to tell you why I'm living how I am. All the couch surfing. Which has to do with all the doctors and the forms."

"Oh!" I say. "Yeah."

Nze looks scared, but takes a breath and rallies. "I'm just gonna show you," she says. She fiddles with the laptop again and turns it to us. It's some kind of list. Across the top it reads, *Bucket List 25*. Then, underneath:

Broadway stage
My dog
Sex, sex, sex
Beach vigil . . .

There's more, but Nze pulls the screen away.

"What's it mean?" Joelle asks. "Bucket List Twenty-Five?"

"It's things I need to do before I turn twenty-five," Nze says. "Because . . ." She looks at the ceiling, back at us. "It's hard to say. Last year, I got this . . . I went in for . . ."

"It's okay, we got you," I say, hitting the just-right tone.

But Nze shakes her head. "That's just it," she says. "I don't want to see your faces get all sad and sympathetic."

"Oh," I say. "Okay, we won't, then." Though I'm not sure how to do that. Or not do it.

Nze nods, blows out air. "Last year I was having trouble seeing at school," she says. "And there's this thing my grandmother had, no big deal, people usually get it when they're old. But the doctor said I had a really rare, bad case of it."

She grips the table and narrows her gaze, studying us. "I'm losing my eyesight," she says. "I could be . . . I could lose it all in not that many years. Like less than ten."

It doesn't really compute. *Blind?* A seventeen-year-old?

"My parents went apeshit," Nze says, shutting down the silence. "They found treatments in Germany and this thing they only do in the Middle East, which my doctor said was shady, but my parents said the doctor didn't like it 'cause it wasn't Western medicine. And how am I supposed to know? I needed to get away from all the shitty choices. I already had enough credits to graduate early, so I did. Now my parents think I'm staying with my cousin, who's covering for me while I couch surf. And work on the bucket list."

She stops talking and looks at us, and I think about how pretty her eyes are and how you don't think about them as working body parts that can quit on you. You just think of how they make you you.

"Wow," Joelle says. "I mean, I'm sorry. Am I allowed to say that?"

Nze rolls her eyes.

"Okay," I say, thinking out loud, because I have to say something. "So, you're being brave as hell. And it makes sense, the bucket list."

"I'm trying to do what feels right," Nze says.

"Speaking of feeling," Joelle says. "Does it hurt? And, your eyes, I mean, how you see—"

"If you hold up two fingers and ask if I can see them . . . ," Nze warns.

Joelle grins and sits on her hands. "Who, me?"

Nze and I laugh, and it's a relief.

"I can see a lot from my left eye," Nze says, "to read and everything. But it's, like, hazy—darker than it should be. I can only see shadows from my right eye. It's less scary than it was at first. Now, I trust what I *am* seeing in a way I didn't when it first started. If that makes sense."

It doesn't, but it sounds like she's coping. And I can tell she wants to stop talking about it. "So, what's next on the list?" I ask. "Can we help?"

"There's a couple things for after the program, like cross the ocean in a boat, somehow. But for this summer . . ." She checks the list. "Next is to look out from a stage on a big audience. I've always wanted to, but I couldn't stand the theater kids in school, so that wasn't gonna happen. I got a gig at the half-price ticket booth, which keeps me up on if there are any calls for extras or anything for Broadway shows. *Anyway*, since it's not just about me, I can add to the list. She types in and shows us the list again. Now the top two items read:

> Find Clae's fairy god somebody
>
> Get Joelle married

"Well, if we're getting me married . . . ," Joelle says, and goes off about her hunt for fancy flowers, cheap.

On the subway back to Mrs. Brisbaine's, I stare at the message *I'll be in touch.* And think about how shitty waiting is. I wonder how Nze can stand it, waiting for darkness to take over.

NINE

BREAKING AND ENTERING

"I'm almost there," Roxy says. Through the phone, I hear a car pass on the street. "You better be sure your mom's not coming home early."

"She's at lunch at Stromboli's. I just texted her," I say. "Are you there? Do you see the flowerpot? The key shouldn't be too deep in the dirt."

"Hang on . . . Yeah, I got it."

"Okay. We're doing this." I sit up straighter on my bed at Mrs. Brisbaine's. Until this second, I didn't really think my plan would work.

I'd gone to bed last night with Nze's doctors, bucket lists, and medical forms on my mind. And I woke up with an idea. No way my nurse mom doesn't have medical records for my dad, if she could get them. And those records might have information, like names of family members. Or . . . if the records are from some prison, somewhere.

I needed to find out. And that meant Roxy.

It wasn't as hard as I thought, calling her and spilling the whole thing. Maybe because I'd already told Nze and Joelle. I admitted that the mystery human at 2200 Flatlands never wrote back to me, but I was too embarrassed to say. And I'm still trying to find them, anyway. "I think there's a secret that my mom doesn't want me to know," I told her. "About my dad. Like maybe he did something worse than blowing off his pregnant girlfriend."

"Why didn't you just tell me all that?" Roxy had asked.

"It's just . . . really sad, isn't it?" I said. "I mean, you have a whole big family."

"And you know what jerks they can be!" she said. "It's better if we tell each other stuff."

"Agreed," I said. "Sorry." And then, I still had to ask for her help. "So . . . could you go to my house and look for something for me? Something that could help me figure out the secret?"

"Sure. You want me to send it to you?"

"Not exactly. The thing is, my mom can't know. You can use the spare key to get in, and then just tell me what you find."

"You want me to break into your house?"

"Pretty much. Well . . . exactly."

And now it's happening. I grab a pillow and hug it to my stomach.

"Okay, I'm inside," Roxy says. "Let's switch to FaceTime." When we do, her face is flushed and windblown, her back to the familiar brown wood of our front door.

"It's super weird being here alone," she says.

"We can make it quick," I say. "Just go into my mom's room."

She moves up the stairs, the camera catching bits and pieces of Mom's Black history gallery. Not for the first time, I wonder what Roxy thinks of all the random Black people interspersed with pictures of me. Finally she's on the landing, turning into Mom's room. She stops in the doorway, and I can see the door to my room behind her . . . open, though I know I shut it when I left.

"Your mom's so neat!" Roxy says. "But I don't like this. What if she finds out I came in here? What if I find sex toys or something?"

"Disgusting, but I'm pretty sure you won't," I say. "Do you see her dresser, how it's got that kind of cabinet on the side instead of a drawer? That's where she keeps her files."

The camera moves again and stops in front of Mom's cabinet.

"Open it and hold the phone so I can see," I say. I'm pressing the pillow so hard, it's thin as paper. I'm sure I'm going to find something that's been in front of my face forever.

Roxy does what I asked. I'm looking at a row of green hanging files with manila folders tucked inside them. I've seen these files a million times, when Mom puts away her tax paperwork, or has to dig out my birth certificate.

"Can you hold it closer?" I ask. "And then move it so I can read the titles on everything?"

She does what I ask. It's alphabetized, of course, everything neatly labeled:

Appliance Manuals
Cape Ann Savings Bank
Gloucester Family Health Center

"Try there," I say.
"Just has an employee handbook," Roxy says.
"Okay, keep going."

Important Documents, Asha
Important Documents, Clae

"Okay, there!"
The camera dips, and I see folders labeled:

Birth Certificate
SS Card

I tell her to keep going, because I've seen those before.

Insurance, Car
Insurance, Home
Medical, Asha
Medical, Clae

"Whoa! That could be it!" My heart thrashes around like it's high tide in my chest. The camera dips into the green folder:

Appendix Removal

Asthma

Covid-19

Roxy checks each file, but it's only visit summaries from doctor appointments. My body slumps with disappointment.

"Your mom takes really good notes," Roxy says.

"Keep going," I tell her.

Real Estate Prospects

Rental Agreement

Taxes, Federal

All the way to

Misc.

"Try that one."

Roxy's fingers move into the file. The only cream-colored folder reads:

RRB

"Looks like more medical stuff," Roxy says, looking inside.

"It . . . *does*?"

"Yeah! It's forms you fill out at the doctor's office. But there's no name. The place where it would be is . . . scratchy, like somebody covered it over, then maybe copied the page. There's an address, but it's . . . in California."

"Send me a picture!" I say. "Make sure you get the whole form. And the folder, too, where it says RRB." I keep talking while I wait. "RRB. I don't know what the second *R*'s about, but it has to be him. Richard Bryant. It's not like Mom would've told me his middle name . . ."

The pics come through. *"Oakland Medical Center, Family Medical History.* A long grid lists medical problems down one side, and has columns for "patient" or "family member." There's a checkmark in the "patient" column next to asthma. *Mother* is written in next to *diabetes type 1* and also *breast cancer. Father* and *Aunt* are next to *hypertension.*

Wow. My dad had asthma, just like me?

I go back to the top of the form. The spot that asks for the patient's name is blank. Like Roxy said. Under it, there's a spot for DOB, filled in with: August 10, 1989. I do the math, and it fits with the date on the high school ring; he would have been eighteen when he graduated. There's something off, though. I look at the date: 1984.

I saw Mom's license last month when she got her new picture. It had a DOB space, just like the form. *June 1, 1987.* So that would make Mom . . . two years older than my dad? But I'd always thought my dad was older, got Mom pregnant when she was young and naive. And now it looks like he was only seventeen when they got pregnant with me . . . and she was nineteen? Instead of a deadbeat dad who ran off to Antigua, he's a teen dad who's somewhere in California?

"Clae? You're frozen." Roxy's voice comes through my phone.

"I'm . . . oh, no. I'm here."

"Did you find what you were looking for?" she asks.

I don't know how to answer. Roxy closes the drawer, and the camera picks up weird angles as she stands up. I'm still reeling from the birthdates. And *California*? I'd never once heard that my dad had lived in California.

"Oh," Roxy says. "There's another folder, open on the bed. Should I look?"

I tell her sure, but she says it's only one of Mom's real estate files. I flip to the next pic on my phone, the folder with the initials *RRB*. My finger slides over the letters—my dad's initials, right across the hall from my bedroom. It's like it took my coming to New York for me to find things that were right in front of my face. I know his birthdate. I know that he lived in California, I can do whole new searches with that information.

"Okay . . . ," Roxy says. "It probably doesn't matter, but there's a printout with a place in Brooklyn in here. It's circled and she's got a note next to it. 'Right across from River Room'—that's what the note says."

"*River* Room?" I ask. "Like . . ." I spell it out. "R-i-v-e-r? Send me a pic." I twist to my nightstand, pull open the drawer, and take out the J. M. Smith High ring. The finger that was just tracing my dad's initials finds the inscription inside: *river*.

Another hit. *Another find.* My pulse speeds up.

"Yeah," Roxy says. "River. Does that mean something?"

I swallow, and let the nervous excitement flow through me. "You know, I think it might."

TEN

BUILDINGS AND BOYS

Mrs. B hands me the jar from the overnight oats, not hiding her sneer. Since breakfast is her jam, she doesn't approve of shortcuts. But Mom and I live on overnight oats, so now they're my comfort food. And I can use the comfort.

Mrs. B. wipes her hands on the dish towel.

"All right, then," she says, and a minute later the front door clicks behind her. I wash and dry the jar, rearrange glasses on the neat shelves. Today's the day I go back to 2200 Flatlands. I'm excited to find more clues, keep my streak going. But an image popped in my head after I got off FaceTime with Roxy. And now I keep on picturing Mom, alone in our empty house, circling apartments for sale in Brooklyn.

The first time I went to summer camp she cyberstalked the town, looked up everything from the hospitals to the bakeries in case camp desserts weren't up to her standards. So, is she stalking me now? Spending all her time virtually exploring Brooklyn while I try to dig up secrets she wants left alone? Guilt tugs at the oats I just downed. But this isn't about her, I remind myself. It's about me and my dad.

In my room, the scrapbook's open on my desk. There are the pics I put in last time I went to Flatlands, and on the opposite page, I copied out the FGS texts, ending with: *I'll be in touch.* I added a printed screenshot of the medical history form and another of the "river room" note. The new leads haven't panned out yet. No hits from *Richard Bryant California arrest records*, at least. But also, nothing from a search of the birthdate.

And then there's River Room.

The address of the "extreme fixer-upper" Mom circled is 38 Sebastian Avenue, Brooklyn, which, according to Maps, is nowhere near 2200 Flatlands, but *is* close to where J. M. Smith High used to be. *River Room* is an arcade on Sebastian Avenue that looks like it could have been there back when my dad was young. After today, River Room will be my next field trip.

My phone vibrates and I fall on my bed to read the text.

Roxy: U probably didn't get urs yet.

In comes a photo of a glittery party invite. It's got a picture of Marley Evans in a gold gown on one side, a *seventeen* on the other, and a big *SASSY* across the top.

Roxy: U have to admit, it's kind of clever, a Sassy 17 party. It's at the yacht club again. A beach overnight.

It's been nice, not thinking about Marley Evans for a while. Or her stupid party.

Roxy: AND. I've got news.

Me: Spill.

In comes another photo. This one's of her, red hair in all its blowout glory. And her face pressed against a goofy-looking guy.

Roxy: I didn't want 2 tell u till I knew it was real. Meet Liam. MY NEW GUY.

I look up, as if there's someone here at Mrs. Brisbaine's who can explain. When there isn't, I write:

Me: Wait. Manager Liam?

Roxy: 😂😂😂 Manager Liam! Can u believe it?

I know the exact expression on Roxy's face. It's the smug look she gets when she's the only one in class who aces a science test. The difference is, that happens a lot. Rox's never the one to get the guy.

Roxy: Marley's party will be my big reveal. So, see? I really need u 2 come.

Right. She'd hate it if I said no now. I owe her anyway after the breaking and entering situation.

Me: Sure. Of course. Wouldn't miss it.

Thinking about Marley's party is enough to push me out the door. I grab my backpack and stuff in my sketchbook and some homework, then get peanut butter crackers and a Dasani from Mrs. B's cabinets. I'm ready to stay all day.

It's 10:30 in the morning when I get off the subway and the neighborhood's even more alive than last time. The stores are open, and people are everywhere on the sidewalks. I scan for my guy pushing his mom in her chair. No sign of them, but there are other possibilities. I stop in front of the locked iron gates and plan my strategy.

"Excuse me." It's a white guy, going into the complex.

I step aside, and he uses his key to get in.

"Would you mind?" I ask, stepping closer. "My grandma lives in there, but she forgot to come down to meet me."

"Oh, for sure!" He holds the gate for me. So much for needing a strategy. Once I'm in, I make for one of the buildings instead of the tai chi green, so I don't look suspicious. He heads in the other direction, and when he's gone, I grab a seat on a bench. This time, I'm on the watch for someone watching me. Could they have seen me from one of the windows? Would they have had to be out here on the green? My eyes shift from one side to the other. *What if they're here right now?* But everybody just seems regular. There's bunches of kids again, and mostly women and old guys on the benches.

Suddenly, I'm in a dark place. Because why, in this bright sunny courtyard where everybody's living their best life, am I skulking around looking for clues that somebody cares about me? If I have an FGS, close enough to see me, close enough to touch, why is everything on the down-low?

Zach's picture lights up my phone. The sight floods me with relief, and I try to shake off the mood as I answer.

"It's pouring here," he says. "So the snack shack's closed. I would've worked anyway. I like the beach in the rain."

"Same," I say, thinking of my cove on wet days. The rest of my bad mood dissolves as his voice brings back the smell, the wind in my face, making me feel safe and free.

"So, lemme hear it," Zach says. "How're the people? New friends, your family?" He says it like it's a normal question for me—*how's your family?*

"I met two girls I really like," I say. But I pull up the FGS text stream and reread the texts, wondering how I would even tell the story. Zach waits.

"Random question," I say, looking around at the windows above. "What do you know about African proverbs? I mean . . . Do you think only African people use them when they talk, or do you think maybe regular American Black people do, too?"

"Proverbs? Like . . . ?"

I read him the one about courage and common sense. And then I remember that Zach's dad is Cape Verdean, which I know is in Africa because he told me once. "For the record, I didn't ask because of your dad," I say.

"Oh. Didn't think you did," he says. "Now you say it, though, my aunt does have this one thing hung next to her toilet." It's quiet a minute while he thinks, then says, "'If the baboon could see his own behind, he'd laugh too.'"

I laugh. "Really? Is she African, this aunt?"

"Yup, that one is. I have every kind of aunt, uncle, cousin." He tells me about the different-colored people in his family, from pale white to dark-skinned Black.

"Cape Verdeans are like that," he says. "Not even counting people marrying other races."

"Wow," I say, impressed at this whole side of him I never knew.

"Yeah, well . . . ," Zach says. Then, since he never keeps the conversation on himself too long: "So, tell me the coolest thing you've done since you've been there."

Right. I look at the kids, who are sitting now, eating ice cream. I think of Brooklyn Bridge Park, pizza, Mr. Barber, and the twenty-seventh floor.

"It's all cool," I say, meaning it. "This place, it's so . . . everything all at once."

"You know, I could come there," Zach says suddenly, in a rush of words. "If you wanted. I could find somewhere to stay, and we could just hang."

"Zach . . ." It's not like I'm not tempted. It would be nice to see him, maybe get drunk again on moonlight and popcorn. And a taste of home. "I guess, yeah," I say.

At that exact second, something makes me look up. Bolt, the boy from the café, is making his way toward me. He's grinning hard. When he stops in front of me, his cuteness is so in my face, it's hard to think.

"Can we talk about it later?" I say to Zach. "I don't . . . know my schedule or anything yet . . ."

"Sure," Zach says. "Just let me know when's good."

I get off quick. Seeing Bolt again makes me feel all kinds of things. Mostly pheromone-related.

"Look at that," he says. "It's next time already." His all-black outfit—jeans, tank, and Vans—is working for him, especially the muscle tank. I wave a hand for him to take the seat next to me, feeling a rush at seeing him right as I was talking to Zach.

"You waiting on your grandma?" Bolt asks, looking around for an old lady.

"She . . . just left," I say.

"I been out here a lot myself," he says. "Seeing how fast next time could come."

He gives me a lopsided grin, smoother than the guy who got his own name wrong. I feel warm all over from the way he looks at me. It's not news that boys like me sometimes. But never cute chocolate-skinned New York City boys. Because I don't know what to say, I try to remember the list I wrote last time I saw him—for in case there was a next time. *It was all about the FGS and how to find number 22 and get inside the building, right?*

I think about how much has changed since that day. First contact. *I'll be in touch* and the African proverbs. Young California Dad and River Room. I decide to ask about the African proverbs I was asking Zach about.

"Random question," I say. "Do a lot of African people live here?"

He looks surprised. "We got a lot of Bajans," he says. "You know, people from Barbados. And there's a guy in my building who wears African-print shorts. He's got an accent, so maybe him."

He squints at me, like, *Why you asking this?*

"My grandma doesn't love her building," I say, surprised at my own easy answer. "I was thinking she might move. She's in apartment number twenty-two."

"Oh, blue building," he says. "I got a friend there, in eight."

Blue building—number 22 is in blue building. My face must light up because Bolt grins back.

"Want to head over to the park?" he asks. "That's where people usually hang."

"Well . . . I still don't really know you," I tell him. "Even though it's 'next time.'"

"Got you," he says. He goes in his bag, pulls out a mini speaker, and puts on some quiet rap. "Where should I start?" he asks. "I'm doing business administration at CUNY. I play the bass. Do six shifts a week at Starbucks, which got me addicted to this stuff called dirty chai. I like the park. Yeah, I still live with my parents, but not for long."

He slips an arm around my shoulder . . . but he doesn't just let it rest there. His warm thick-fingered hand closes on my arm, slides up to my shoulder and back again, causing a lot of tingling that goes way past my arm and makes me forget about blue building, at least for a minute. I think of Zach, though, then tell myself it's all good. There's no reason I can't hang out with Bolt.

The ice cream guy comes by, and we get ICEEs. When I don't start eating mine, Bolt takes it out of my hand and feeds me bites from the tiny spoon.

"How come it tastes better this way?" I ask.

"All about the messenger," he says.

Okay, yeah. I like this guy. And I want him to help me figure out this place. *And* I like Zach, too . . .

When Bolt goes to throw out our empty cups, I watch blue building again. From what I see, you don't need a key to get in the front door, but there's a second locked door across the entryway. Bolt comes back. He sits a little closer, but he doesn't start talking again, which is nice, with his music giving us background sound.

"You smell good," Bolt says.

He's leaning in, maybe sniffing my neck? I like it. But I turn away because I don't know what he's planning, and I'm not trying to kiss him right now. And that's when I see them. Two women walking to the door of blue building, both wearing bright African wrap skirts. One of them's old enough to be my grandma. The younger one turns to laugh at something the other one said. She has a nice face, warm and open. I watch as they disappear through the door.

"*What?*" Bolt asks.

"I don't know," I say, looking from the women down to my phone, which seems to represent Zach right now. It's a lot, two boys into me and a possible FGS sighting, all at once. But not in a bad way.

I give Bolt my best flirty smile. "I don't know *yet,*" I amend. "I guess we'll find out, though."

ELEVEN

SKIN IN THE GAME

"We should go over our pitch one more time," I say to Nze and Joelle. "This is our one major project for class, and we didn't practice enough!"

We're in the classroom on the twenty-seventh floor, waiting for our mentor session with Mr. Barber. Nze's messing with her hair, which she's got in pigtails, Afro-puff style. Joelle's deep in a screenful of flowers, her magenta cap pulled low, her matching lips poked out in concentration.

My palms are sweating. I'm grateful they took my pitch idea, which I came up with to help me find out more about my dad's high school. And we did some half-decent research, but I'm not sure if Mr. Barber will like the idea.

"Come on, let's go!" I say again.

But too late. Mr. Barber strides in, grabs a desk, and pulls it around to sit in front of us. He's got on a bright blue jacket and black shirt, and he rubs his hands together, beaming like he's face-to-face with one of Mrs. Brisbaine's biscuits. Nze and Joelle finally look up.

"Talk!" Mr. Barber says. "What brilliant seeds have sprouted from your young minds?"

"We definitely have some ideas," I say.

"Absolutely!" Nze says. "Clae's gonna start us off."

"Great, great," Mr. Barber says.

All their eyes settle on me.

"We want to do a feature story," I say. "Taking a current hot topic and giving it backstory, history, and analysis. The hot topic is what people are calling 'anti-woke education'—like how they're trying to shut down teaching Black history in schools. We found out about these schools called Black Freedom Schools, which have been a way that Black people have been fighting for better, historically accurate education, like, forever. Even during enslavement. So our thing is that what's happening now is just same old same old. And that's what our article would explore."

"I have a cousin in Florida," Nze chimes in, "who says lots of people are doing homeschooling there now because of how the government's banning accurate textbooks. And it's nothing new. The Black Freedom Schools were like the original homeschools, with parents and community teachers getting together to make the curriculum and pay for everything."

"*But*," Joelle says. "It's not always roses and puppy dogs. Some Black-run schools have been harsh . . . So we're doing analysis. Lots of sides to the story."

"Do I look impressed?" Mr. Barber says. He's grinning ear to ear, and it's all I can do not to groan with relief.

"What sparked your interest in this topic?" he asks, eyes glistening at us.

Again, Nze and Joelle turn to me.

"I, um . . . my dad went to a Freedom School," I say. "When I looked it up, I found out that it's a whole thing from way way back. Even my dad's school, it had like this old African saying for its motto. So it was like it was connecting to the schools that they had here in New York even during enslavement."

"Your dad did? Where was this?"

"Here. Or, I guess, Brooklyn. The J. M. Smith High School. Did you ever hear of it?" I hold my breath a little.

"Can't say as such," Mr. Barber says. "But would it be named after the great James McCune Smith, our first Black doctor and an education leader in New York? An interesting figure, worthy of having a school named for him."

I'm already typing it into my laptop. "McCune, did you say? Wow, it is him!" I scan the search page. The term *James McCune Smith High School* brought up a full page of entries, a ton more than when I just put in the initials.

"Very good," Mr. Barber says. "*Indeed.* And do you have your outline ready for me? Including candidates to interview and research plans, ensuring a healthy mix of facts, analysis, and quotes from people affected?"

"All set," Nze says. "We just wanted to talk to you before we submitted it."

He hands us each our folder and tells us to read his comments on the essays we wrote to get into the program, so we can "build on strengths and learn from errors."

"We meet again on Monday," he says, opening his arms wide. "Anything else for now?"

We shake our heads, and he gives us an actual wink. "I expect great things from the three of you," he says before he leaves.

"He liked it!" I say, letting my head fall back on my chair. "Phew! *And* he gave us a name for the high school guy."

"*And* we're done!" Joelle says. "Finally, we get to go to my room. I'm about to blow your minds!" She jumps out of her seat, bouncing in flat sandals that show off her toe rings.

Now that the hard part's over, I let excitement sink in for our next move—Joelle's surprise that's supposed to help me understand the FGS. We leave the building and cross a short street. It's not long before we stop in front of a huge building with wide steps, tall glass doors, and columns on either side. It looks like the front of a college brochure, and it gives me gooseflesh. I step back and take it in.

This is the dream. If I ace the program, I could get a scholarship that would let me live someplace like this.

Joelle uses a key card to let us into a big polished entry hall. We go up on the elevator, then down a narrow linoleum-tiled hallway.

"Give me a sec to get it ready," Joelle says, stopping at a door with a flowery *Joelle* nameplate.

She unlocks it and slips inside, but there isn't much time before the door opens again.

"Come!" she says, ushering us in. Instantly I know why she wanted to go in first. There are lit candles on her dresser and desk and on a low table in the middle of the floor that's got snacks and a teapot on it, and three pillows arranged like chairs. The back wall has a long clothes rack that's draped with white fabric—lacy, silky, creamy, all knotted over the rack and draping down to the floor.

"Get comfy," Joelle says, pointing to the pillows. I pick a crimson-colored one that puts me with my back to the window and nab a mini can of Pringles. I love the room, not because I'd decorate like this but because it feels so much like Joelle. Even my room at home isn't this much me.

"What I'm going to tell you," Joelle says, taking a seat and pouring three paper cups of tea. "Isn't even what I was planning to share for my secret thing. But I think it can really help you, Clae. So here it is." She does a serious dramatic pause, looking from one of us to the other. "I'm an empath. A really good one. Especially here in my own space when it's cleansed and ready for me."

"Do you mean like in sci-fi?" Nze asks. "Where empaths can take other people's pain away?"

"Hard no," Joelle says. "I'm just really tuned into feelings and energy, even through a computer or cell phone. Here, look." She pulls up something on her phone and holds it out. "You play this?"

"It's my mom's favorite," I say, checking out the Wordle puzzle she's pulled up. It has the word *FRANK* in a single row of green letters, which means it was solved in one try.

"I *always* win," Joelle says. "Because I can feel whoever programmed the thing. One try, two tops, *every time*. That's how I can help with your fairy god whatever. I can tell stuff about them from their texts."

"That is . . . *wow*," Nze says. "But go on, do one of the Wordle things, so we can see."

Joelle scowls at her. "That's actually a big thing about empathy—as an empath you have to trust yourself. And you all need to trust me, too."

"But how's it empathy?" I ask. "Are you saying you can feel the FGS's feelings, and from that you can tell who they are?" I think it's bullshit, but I can't help asking.

Joelle gets up and pulls down the window shade, so the room goes gold and flickery from the candles. There's a smell, I notice now, like honey and grass. Nze's expression says, *This is gonna be good, whether it helps you or not.*

"Just trust me, okay?" Joelle says, sitting back down. "When you're ready, Clae, open your phone to your person's text and give it to me. I'll tell you what I feel." She sits, Buddha calm, palm up for my phone.

Not looking at Nze, I open the text stream and hand it over, because it's not like anything else I've tried has worked. Joelle scrunches her face and concentrates on the messages. *Hard.* Her expression is focused and open at the same time. I lean forward to catch her every move. After a minute, I glance at Nze, who nods. Even she's buying it.

Finally, Joelle glances up.

"Can you tell anything?" I ask.

"I can tell a lot," she says. "Whoever they are, they've got skin in the game. They *care.* When they wrote this, they weren't just like, *whatever.* It was intense for them."

92

My heart literally flutters. *They care.* "They care . . . about me?" I ask.

"It's complicated," Joelle says. "I'd say her feelings are mostly positive. But there's stress, too. Worry . . ."

It's hard to take everything in. They care about me, but . . . "Wait. *Her?*" I say. "You said *her.* How do you . . . ?"

"It feels like a woman," Joelle says with a shrug.

"But Mom said my dad had a brother, no sister! So does that mean it has to be a grandma? Can you tell if they're old?"

"Sorry, no," Joelle says, her face finally relaxing into a smile. "But that's a lot what I got, right?"

I nod. Definitely a lot.

"Okay," Joelle says. "So, what now? What do you want to have happen?"

"What do you mean?" I ask. "I want them to come clean already and tell me who they are and why they never showed their face and what they're hiding!" I feel flushed.

Joelle beams at me, nodding.

"I want to know where the trail leads. What Uncle Wendell wanted me to find."

"So, how do we get her to tell you all that?" Nze asks, looking from Joelle to me.

"What do you think I've been trying to do?" I ask. "I'm asking! She's not answering!"

"Okay, but remember what I said about trusting yourself," Joelle says. "What you feel for and from this person got you all the way here. So you have to ask yourself, are you acting on that connection?

93

Are you trusting what you feel and acting on it?"

"What I feel?" I say. "What I feel is pissed. Super pissed!" I don't know what that has to do with empathy, but saying it makes the anger bubble up even more.

"And what does that anger make you want to say to her?" Joelle asks.

I take a long breath of the honey-and-grass air, looking around at the candlelit room. *What do I want to say to the FGS?* Very slowly—so there's no chance I'll hit send by accident—I type a message.

Me: I want the truth. Are you related to me? Are you related to my father?

"This is nuts," I say, turning the phone to show them.

"It's perfect," Joelle says.

"She's right," Nze says. "She just is. Hit send."

I look at them, then back at my simple, true message. I still don't get the empathy thing, but something about asking the hard question feels good. Real. Like I'm in it, not just sitting on the sidelines whispering and hoping.

So I hit send.

We sit in silence, and I know they get what a big deal it is. I take some more breaths and slump back on my pillow.

"Wow," Nze says. "That might not have been total bullshit."

Joelle throws a Pringle at her.

And then there's a *ding. And it's my phone.*

Unknown: Do not think the lion is asleep just because it is not roaring. Such is the danger of making assumptions.

"Assumptions?" I whisper. "What . . . ?"

And then, another *ding*.

Unknown: It is probably best to discuss in person. Shall we meet on Thursday?

Ding.

Unknown: The Checkerboard Bistro on University Place?

"Damn, damn, damn!" Nze says, while Joelle beams like a proud mama. "We'll be done with classes by three on Thursday. Say you can be there at four. We can get there early and get you set up."

I could have a grandma on Thursday? My stomach leaves my body at the thought.

"Just say yes," Nze says. "Finish it."

I type that I can meet her at four.

And a thumbs-up pops up on my screen.

TWELVE

GRANDMA/NOT GRANDMA

I think about it on the train back to Mrs. Brisbaine's.

On Thursday, I'll meet the FGS, who, now that Joelle says it's a woman, I think of as Grandma/Not Grandma. She'll be sitting across from me in some random restaurant. I can ask her all the questions. The little-girl ones I've been waiting all this time to ask. And the *What the hell?* ones I have now.

What will she be like? Is she *old-old*? Is she the woman in the African skirt?

Does she know where my dad is?

On the walk to Mrs. Brisbaine's, I call Zach because talking to him pulled me out of my funk at 2200 Flatlands.

"Something happened," I say. "Something scary—not like mugger scary. Just . . ."

"Okay. You wanna tell me what?"

"No."

"Oh. Want me to distract you? Or, I could make you laugh. I saw this . . ."

I tune him out. The sound of his voice is all I need, and I like that he didn't try to make me tell him what happened. I wonder how he stays so steady.

"How do you keep from freaking out about things?" I ask, cutting off whatever he's saying. "You just stay so chill. Is it your family, or . . . ?"

"I just find people I like," he says. "And when they're not around, I hang at the water."

"Yeah." I think of my cove again. For the first time, I wish something from Gloucester were here.

"What do *you* do to not freak out?" Zach asks.

Talking to you works, I think. But I'm not ready to tell him that.

"Still working on it," I say. "Anyway, I'm here, at Mrs. Brisbaine's."

I hang up, feeling confused about what's happening with Zach. Am I supposed to tell him that other boys are smelling my neck?

By the time I get up the walkway, I'm back to thinking about the FGS. Sounds from the TV meet me at the door as I let myself inside.

"You good, Mrs. B?" I ask, sticking my head in to see her, all cozy in her nest. She gives me her vague nod, which is my cue to disappear into my room for the rest of the night. But the only thing I know right now is that being alone isn't it. I go in my room, take out my contacts, and put on my glasses, because if I have to cry later, it'll be easier. I grab my sketchbook and pencils to keep my hands busy and head back out. When I get to the door, I stop, turn around, and take the ring Uncle Wendell gave me and slip it on my thumb. Then I go back to the TV room.

"Mrs. B? Can I watch with you?"

She's so surprised she actually looks away from the TV. "Come on, then," she says.

I go to the far end of the couch and settle down. I feel like I shouldn't ask what she's watching, just shut up and figure it out. It doesn't take long to see it's some syrupy feel-good show.

"*Touched by an Angel*," Mrs. B. says, and just saying it puts a smile on her face. Angels and breakfast are her love languages, apparently. On the TV, old-fashioned people are looking sad to violin music. I pull out my phone, text Roxy a *wassup?*, but she doesn't answer.

I look back at the TV. Of course the perfect Grandma/Not Grandma is there, on the screen. She's round and brown with nice eyes and a lot of bold grandma energy. She reminds me of a picture we have of Mom's mom, Grandma Sarah, before she died. It's not a great photo, but you can tell she was round at least. Uncle Wendell managed to tell one story about Grandma Sarah. Barely a story, but better than nothing. Mom was braiding my hair for me one night in the living room, and Uncle Wendell said to her, "You remember how hers was? Momma's?"

I noticed that Mom's fingers didn't go rigid or anything. I kept breathing the same as I had been. Uncle Wendell kept talking.

"That long black hair she had," Uncle Wendell said. "You could tell she had some Indian in her."

"Everybody has some something in them," Mom said. And that was it. Her fingers tightened on my braid, and she changed the subject.

Twirling the ring on my thumb, I glance at Mrs. Brisbaine, who has forgotten I'm here. Joelle was right about it being good to act on your feelings. I think about Mom and Uncle Wendell and how she always shut him down when he talked about the past. And why didn't we ever visit him, where he lived? I grab my phone and text Mom. No hi. Just:

Me: Why didn't we see more of Uncle Wendell?

As usual, if she's not at work, she answers right away.

Mom: What's this about?

Keeping half an eye on the TV grandma, I write:

Me: Saw someone who looked like him today.

This time she doesn't answer right off. TV Grandma/Not Grandma says wise things to a white woman while Mrs. Brisbaine nods slowly in agreement. I keep glancing at my phone, but I'm glad Mom's having a hard time with what I sent.

Finally, she answers.

Mom: I miss him, too, especially now when I'm missing you. When I was little, he was the only one who would play with me for hours. He was a good big brother.

Wha . . . ? Why didn't she say that to him when he was alive? She writes:

Mom: How are your classes? I know you're doing great.

I sigh and give in to the queen of changing subjects. I tell her about Mr. Barber liking our proposal. Her praise feels nice, of course, and I let her go on until Roxy writes back. Except Roxy has crazy news, too.

Roxy: Did u hear about Marley's girlfriend?

Instantly, I know what she means, even though I hadn't heard anything.

Roxy: Did u know?

Me: No. Not really.

Roxy: She just started showing up places with this girl Maya. I saw them at the shop holding hands.

Joelle must be rubbing off on me because I feel a hundred percent sure Maya's Black, just from reading the text. I wonder where Maya goes to school, where Marley met her. It's like Marley's having a whole other kind of Black-girl adventure this summer, while I have mine with Nze and Joelle.

Me: Good for Marley.

Roxy: I know.

Me: Gotta go.

I toss my phone down and shuffle through memories for clues. *Did* I know Marley liked girls? All those years of parties, of our moms dragging us to museums or Black movies together. No clues . . . so, why do I feel like I should've known?

"Just beautiful," Mrs. Brisbaine says, as credits roll on the screen. "Now, let's see what's next." She picks up the remote, clicks, and sits back to get comfy as more smarmy music plays. I try to shake off my Marley Evans weirdness and wonder how I'm supposed to survive this night, let alone two more before I meet the FGS.

On-screen, some girls lay out sleeping bags and squeal as the doorbell rings. If Nze's couch surfing, anyway . . .

Me: Can u stay at my place Wednesday night?

Nze: Thought you couldn't have people over on a "school" night?

Me: We won't be asking.

Nze: Cool

I stay where I am until Mrs. B's show ends. After agreeing that it was *a whole lotta fun*, I say, "Before I forget, we have a late seminar Wednesday night. I'll try to make it back by ten, but it may be a little after."

"I close down at ten o'clock," she reminds me, already over her angel glow. "I can't be up late, now."

"I know!" I say, like I've been worrying about that, too. "You should get in bed, and I'll knock on your door the second I'm in, okay? I promise it won't be late."

She lets me know it better not be, which is good enough. Mrs. B's been in bed at ten every night since I got here. So on Wednesday, I'll come in a little after she's down, stick my head in so she knows I'm here. Then I'll give her a few minutes to fall asleep and let Nze in for our sleepover.

So that'll get me from Wednesday to Thursday. Now, I just have to make it through tomorrow.

THIRTEEN

RIVER TO RIVER

> Me: What are u doing this afternoon? Want to go to an arcade
> with me?
>
> Bolt: I get off at 2.
>
> Me: Meet me at Sebastian Ave, Brooklyn. River Room.

An hour later, I stare in the dull gray mirror in the single-stall bathroom of River Room. A girl in glasses looks back at me. I *never* wear
my glasses out in Gloucester. So . . . why did I decide to wear them
on a sort-of date, even if it is to a grungy arcade?

Someone knocks. I call, "In a sec," and leave my reflection for
the job I'm supposed to be doing. There's plenty of graffiti on the
gray walls. I start at the top above the toilet and work my way across
and down. No *RB* or *RRB*. No *RB* and *AM*, tucked inside a heart.
Not a surprise, really, but I'm still disappointed. I unlock the door

and leave, passing a white kid with black glasses like mine.

The arcade's dark and smells of melted cheese and never-cleaned floors. There are two rooms: driving and shooting games in front, and old-school arcade stuff in back. Kids my age and younger chow on chicken poppers, Tater Tots, and grilled cheese sandwiches. I look for people who work here and see a guy behind the food counter, way too young to remember my dad, and a person cleaning up in the back room, who looks old. I watch him sweep. What would I ask him? Do you remember a kid named Richard from seventeen years ago? I'm not sure what he looked like, but maybe kinda like me . . . ?

"Hola." It's Bolt, coming up behind me.

"Oh, hi!" I say. "You made it."

"'Course," he says. Then, touching my glasses, he adds, "You look great."

I smile big, liking the compliment and glad to see him.

Bolt looks around. "I didn't know you were into stuff like this. What's your game?"

I decide to just hang for a minute, worry about finding clues later. "Where I'm from, we're all about the Skee-Ball," I say.

"You'll still like me when I beat you, right?" he says, leading the way.

It's the kind that takes quarters. We both get change from the machine, and Bolt sets up the first round, then stands back for me to go. He looks good in a blue hoodie and jeans, his hair on-purpose messy. Something about his energy—that little touch to my glasses—tells me this is a date on his end. I wonder what Zach would think, if he knew. Okay, I know what he would think.

I flub the first ball and get ten points.

Bolt nails a forty. I close my eyes and block out everything but the little alley in front of me. I like winning. And I like being here with him.

I get the fifty!

"We'll see about that," Bolt says. He gets another forty.

"That's your strategy?" I ask. "Just aim for the forty every time. Don't you think it's kind of chickenshit to not even *try* for the fifty or hundred?"

I aim for the hundred in the left corner. And get it!

"It's like that?" he says, eyes bulging like he's wounded. "Fine." He makes a big deal of aiming and . . . lands a ten.

"See?" I say, giggling. "Much better strategy!" He twists his lips, says the game's not over yet.

I get a thirty, a fifty, two tens—when I was shooting for the hundred—and a twenty. Bolt sticks with his forties, until we're at our last ball.

It's 280 me, and 290 Bolt. If he lands a forty and I land a fifty, we're tied. I have to go for the hundred if I want to win.

I tell him to stand back, and I mean it. No looking over my shoulder and messing me up. I want to win bad, but there's still a goofy smile on my face. I hone in on the hundred in the left pocket, the same one I made before. And . . . nail it!

Bolt groans. Forty's a losing game for him now, he can only win with a hundred. He lines up the shot and . . . gets a twenty. I win!

"All right, all right," he says. "We just got started, and I got a lotta quarters."

I tell him I don't have all night because I'm meeting Nze and Joelle later. I don't tell him they planned a surprise night for me, to keep me from losing it about the FGS on Thursday.

"You'll get your rematch," I say. "After I'm done feeling my *first* victory."

"While it lasts," he says. "You hungry?"

I am, so we order two grilled cheeses with Tater Tots and sit on stools at the counter to wait, Bolt with his hands in his pockets and his body leaned toward mine. I look around, and the old guy's still there, standing around with his broom.

"I know it's a little weird," I tell Bolt. "But I think my dad used to hang out here. I'm gonna ask, see if any of the older people remember him."

"Yeah? Did he . . . ?"

"Die?" I ask, getting what he means. "No . . . Well, I don't think so. He left when I was a baby, so . . ."

Bolt gives a slow nod. He looks away from me. I'm not sure why, but I don't like it.

"What?" I ask.

He shrugs, but doesn't answer. Our food comes, but I keep my eyes on him. I want to hear what he has to say.

"It's just, I got a cousin," he says, "Who's in that same situation— dad left when she was little. And now she's obsessed with how life was back when he was home. She's got all these sad little-kid memories, like those were the good old days and nothing can ever be as good again."

"So, you're saying . . . ?"

"Maybe it's better not getting caught up in the people who left."

My eyebrows sink. My heart rate goes way up.

"Just my opinion," Bolt says.

I'm not sure why I'm so mad, but I am. Bolt takes a huge bite of his sandwich and keeps himself busy chewing.

"Back in a minute," I mumble. I head back toward the Skee-Ball for someplace to be and stand behind a couple by the window.

It's better not getting caught up in the people who left. It's *not* Bolt's business but it still hurts. It's not like it's fun, wanting people who don't want me back. So, am I just gonna turn out miserable, like his cousin, *obsessed* with something I can never have?

The couple in front of the window moves, and I step up. The river's not that close, a stretch of sparkly blue, surrounded by concrete. I wonder if my dad used to stand here and look at it, like I look at my cove at home. And I wish I knew. I wish I understood why he left. Is that so bad? Or is Bolt right? And Mom. Am I wasting my time, pissing Mom off, betraying her even, for nothing?

I go eat cold greasy Tots with Bolt, but we don't get back the good energy from before. He plays driving games, and I check out the old-school machines in case there's some sign. The guy with the broom's gone, and I'm mad I missed my chance with him. When we go back to Skee-Ball, we tie, both of us with lower scores.

"I'm not obsessed," I say, when the game's over.

"Huh?"

"It's not that I'm obsessed with my dad. I know it's shitty that he left. And my mom did a great job raising me. I'm proud of her. I get that single moms can do it."

"Yeah," he says. "Got you."

"It's more about my dad's family," I say. "I could have aunts and uncles, cousins, and grandparents. I want to find out about all of *them*."

"I understand," he says.

"'Kay. It's time for me to go meet my friends."

Bolt grabs my hand. "I was just trying to help," he says. He swings my arm until I look at him. "What about later? My band's practicing tonight. You could pull up with your friends."

I'm about to say no, because of my curfew, plus I have class tomorrow, and I'm still mad.

But he says, "It's by your grandma's, at my friend's place. In blue."

Blue building? At 2200 Flatlands? I picture myself inside that building, and I don't care what Bolt says. Or Mom. I could walk right up to the door and knock. The door would open. And I'd *know*.

"We go for hours," Bolt says. "You can come whenever."

A part of me thinks, *No, don't do it! The FGS'll be mad.* I should wait till Thursday like we planned. But a chance to be inside 2200 Flatlands, to knock on that door?

"Sounds fun," I say. "We'll be there."

"Close your eyes," Nze says an hour later, as we head up the subway stairs at the Times Square stop. She slides a hand over my eyes and another behind my back. Joelle puts a hand on my shoulder, and they walk me up a bunch of stairs and out into open air again.

107

"Okay, now!" Nze lifts her hand. Every inch of space is full of light and bodies and noise. Neon blares from every direction, theater marquees and ads for plays—*Hamilton, Moulin Rouge, SIX, Wicked, The Lion King.* Massive hotels break up blocks of smaller shops all hawking something lit up or loud or greasy-smelling.

"It's always like this?" I ask. "Every day?"

"Every day, like this," Nze says.

She grabs my hand and Joelle takes the other one, and we have to push through walls of people in order to move. I thought it would be impossible not to think about seeing the FGS tonight, but it's more impossible not to pay attention to where I am.

Nze's in her happy place, giving me a Broadway tour. "Down there's where I work." She points. "The half-price ticket line. Even at half price, though, it's way too expensive. Oh, and look! *Paradise Square!* It's the best Black musical out right now! "

The play's name is all lit up on the marquees over the theater and a ripped Black guy's leaning against the golden theater doors, dressed in tight jeans and a plain white tee. He raises his coffee cup to us.

"I bet he's one of the dancers," Nze whispers. She smooths her jeans and rests a hand on her boobs. "Do you dare me to go over?"

"Sure," I say at the same time Joelle says, "No way!"

Nze gives her a dirty look. "Have you noticed what's not getting any play on my list?"

"Right!" I say. "Sex."

"It doesn't just say sex," Nze corrects. "It says *sex, sex, sex.* That's for quantity, quality, and . . . variation."

Joelle raises her eyebrows. "What's variation mean?"

"I'm not sure," Nze says, looking embarrassed but stubborn. "But whatever it is, I wanna try it while I can see all the body parts."

"Yeah, well, we're on a schedule," Joelle says. "You can find variety sex on your own time."

Nze rolls her eyes but agrees. We go another few blocks, and Nze points out stage doors, the best plays, and a huge store that sells nothing but M&M'S. Then we turn onto a side street that's a little less packed than where we've been so far. A woman's staked out the corner with blankets and bags spread out and a glass jar to collect money.

"Hang on," Joelle says. She fishes a five-dollar bill out of her bag and drops it in the jar.

"Have a nice day," she tells the woman. Then to us: "I thought this city was so dangerous from how my mom acted when I was little. We weren't even allowed to talk to people on the street. But then when I started going places with Chaz, I realized that was just her. That's how she is."

"How's how she is?" I ask. I've been wondering about Joelle's mom since I heard about the ambush wedding.

"Always thinking everybody's bad and out to get her. Which is just, like this huge *irony*, because she *picks* terrible people, and then she trashes good people for no reason."

"Like Chaz?" Nze asks. "Is that the deal with the wedding? She doesn't like your guy?"

Joelle responds by putting an arm around each of us. "I'll tell you when we get there," she says. "The pond's the perfect place to talk."

Half an hour later, I realize the pond's in Central Park, which is so big, it's like someone dropped a country town in the middle of the city. Once we're inside, the noises of cars, hawkers, and crowds die away. We walk past climbing rocks and little-kid play apparatuses, and then Joelle points to a wide pond with a grassy bank.

"It's where Chaz and I sat on our first date. He brought champagne and bananas and hot dogs and chocolate chip cookies. He even picked up a frog for me to pet."

"You two really were made for each other," Nze says.

Joelle totally misses the sarcasm as she spreads out a cotton blanket she'd tucked in her bag. "The park we'll be at for the wedding picnic isn't as nice as this, but we're going to have blankets like this one, for nostalgia. And we're going to sneak in some hot dogs and bananas just for us, even though the rest of the food'll be what my mom likes."

She has that tone again that she gets when she talks about her mom. Distant and colder than usual.

"So, tell us now," I say. "What you wanted to say about your mom."

Joelle nods, absently taking more supplies out of her bag. She's got mini water bottles, a sleeve of crackers, those tiny tins of cheese spread, plus a box of Double Stuf OREOs.

"Here's the thing with my mom," she says. "Nutshell version. She and my dad split when I was seven. They both got remarried quick. Then Mom had my little sister, and they're like peas in a pod. Them and my stepdad, they're very . . . proper. All about doing the right thing, looking the right way, having the right friends."

"Right for what?" I ask.

"Other fancy Black people. Who go to fancy Black places and own fancy things, like first editions of Langston Hughes and Jacob Lawrence originals." She holds up a hand. "Not that those are bad things. And my mom's amazing and elegant and smart. It's just that stuff's all she's into. And me marrying a *white* guy who doesn't even care about his own family's money? Which even I get is a way white thing to do." She stops to breathe, then plows on. "And then Chaz, he's . . . you met him, he's gonna seem all *performative* to her, even though that's not who he is at all. And that leaves me in this lousy spot, because I want Mom to be into our marriage, but I can't tell her in advance because I know she'll try and stop me. It's a *lot* of pressure."

"But how's the wedding going to help?" I ask. Because it seems like the wedding will make it worse. "If she's not into your getting married and she doesn't like Chaz . . . ?"

Joelle lights up. "That's just it, I'm gonna *prove* how right it is at the wedding. The flowers, the food will all help. But especially *the dress*!"

"Come again?" Nze says.

"She needs to see that I'm still who she raised!" Joelle says. "Words can't show her, but the perfect dress can. She'll see that I still love beautiful things and I have great taste and she'll . . . *melt*."

That makes no sense to me, but luckily some frogs ribbit so loud that we all laugh. One of them plops into the pond. I change the subject, slightly.

"What about your dad?" I ask. "And the rest of your family . . .

like if you have aunts and uncles or cousins."

"They'll be mad I cheated them out of a wedding," she says with a shrug. "But my dad'll be fine. And my cousin in Philly'll throw us a party afterward."

"Must be nice," I say, thinking what it would feel like to piss off one family member and know all these other people would still be there for you.

Nze and Joelle both look at me.

I fill them in on how Bolt made me feel bad for wanting to know about my dad and his family. "I told him it wasn't like that," I say. "I'm not some desperate daddy's girl. My mom rocked the single-mom thing. But, if I'm real. . . I do want to know about my dad, even though he left us."

Nze and Joelle make encouraging noises, letting me know it's okay to want what I want.

"It's the first thing I'm gonna ask the FGS," I say. "Then I'll know what happened to him, and I can focus on the rest of his family. I mean, *my* family. Whoever they are." I feel embarrassed, just saying the words *my family* about anybody other than Mom and Uncle Wendell.

"Good for you," Nze says. "Black families are the best. Even though mine's out of control right now."

I don't say how it's always hurt to be around other people's big Black families, or how Marley Evans rubbed hers in my face our whole lives.

When we start to pack up, Nze, who's been on her phone, says, "Hold up. Pull out your phones. I have presents for you."

Joelle's comes through first, and she squeals. I look over her shoulder and see:

Nze: Joelle and her Chaz

Hot dogs cookies and champagne

This is how love tastes

Joelle says she wants to put it on a T-shirt. Mine comes through:

Nze: Loyalties confused

History's a mystery

Shouldn't have to guess

"Pretty much nailed it," I say.

"Last stop on this fantasmical tour of New York City," Joelle says a while later, as we get off the subway again. "Is the Staten Island Ferry. The trip over's not much. It's all about the trip *back*, when it's dark and you see the city. Plus, it's free."

There's not much to the ferry, just benches and a snack bar with Formica tables and chairs. We get a bench on the outer deck, where we can feel the wind. As we wait to get moving, we plan what we'll do later tonight, once we're finally inside blue building at 2200 Flatlands.

"Ferry's always on schedule," Joelle says, as the boat pulls away. I close my eyes and try to relax to the boat's rocking motion. It's been a long day.

I get a text from Roxy.

Roxy: Remember how I didn't like Liam at first? It was bullshit—I mean, yes, he's 2 into the rules. But I think I liked him right off and I didn't want 2. He's such a nerd.

Me: So?

I don't say *you're such a nerd*, but we both know she is.

Roxy: He plays golf, for Chrissakes.

Me: So???

Roxy: He's also super short. Am I an asshole?

Me: u're an asshole in love 😊

Something about the way she talks about Liam makes me think she really is. I wonder what *that* feels like. I look at Joelle, who I guess I could study for the answer. Or just ask. But I leave it alone.

A text comes in from Zach. It's a picture of the beach where he works the snack shack.

Zach: Miss it?

I do. And him. Since I'm looking out at the water now, too, I take a picture and send it to him.

Me: NYC has everything.

Zach: Nice, but not exactly the open ocean

Me: Boats beat beaches.

Which I don't believe, but what the hell.

Zach: 💀

Zach: I see your boat and raise you a beach.

He sends a picture of a next-level gorgeous beach. There's a link to a Connecticut beach site, with directions to get there on a commuter train from NYC.

Zach: Halfway between here and NYC. Pick you up at the station a week from Sunday?

"Believe it or not," Joelle says, startling me. "We're almost there. We won't even get to Flatlands that late."

"Right," I say. I was so busy thinking about Zach, I'd actually forgotten about the rest of the night. I send up a quick prayer that the broken-down subway excuse I have planned for Mrs. B flies. Then, I read Zach's text again. Next Sunday. I'll've met the FGS by then, for sure. Who knows what might be happening? Including with Bolt, giver of advice nobody asked for. Which puts Zach ahead in the Zach/Bolt competition that's happening in my head.

All at once, the engine cuts and the motion stops. We're still.

"Stay put," Joelle says. "We'll head back in a minute. Remember, it's all about what happens when we pull back into the city."

And after that, I think, we'll go to 2200 Flatlands. And see Bolt. And maybe the FGS.

I think of Roxy and Liam, all cozy in Gloucester, and Zach and me in our boat. And then me here, in Time Square, at school. In Joelle's dorm. With Bolt at River Room. New York Clae is real. And she's moving me farther and farther away, like this boat. And I want to go. But . . .

I text Zach.

Me: Sure. Why not?

A few minutes later, the engine kicks on again and the boat rocks us back toward the city. Almost no one's on board now except us. Darkness falls, making the dampness on my skin tingle as I read excited texts from Zach.

When we're almost to the terminal, Nze says, "Okay, one more time." And she slips a hand over my eyes again. "This one's even better than Times Square."

They march me up by the railing and twist me around to what they say is the perfect spot.

"On three," Nze says. "One. Two. Three!" She moves her hand, and I open my eyes.

The whole city, skyscrapers and bridges, streetlights and billboards, is lit up in neon blue and bright gold, warm white and soft red, right there in front of me, like a pop-up card I'm sailing into.

"It's . . . ," I begin.

"Toldja," Joelle says.

FOURTEEN

MY SOUL ANTICIPATING

It's raining when Bolt meets us at the gate. It's good to see him and nice when he leans down and kisses my cheek. But now that I'm here, I'm all about the FGS tonight. The walkways are empty, and the rain leaves an eerie sort of gleam. Lights are on in most of the windows, but there's a lonely feel to the place. I get more nervous with every step.

"Was this a bad idea?" I whisper to Nze as Bolt opens the inner door of blue building. There's no reception desk or anything, just a long corridor with elevators and numbered apartment doors.

The sound of drumming meets us before we get to Bolt's friend's door, the second to last one on the first floor. I see there's ten apartments per floor. Number twenty-two is on the third floor, I calculate.

"Help yourself to food and drinks," Bolt says when we go in.

We're in a dimly lit living room with the band set up on one end and five or six people on a couch and matching chairs. A coffee table's cluttered with random food and bottles. Bolt points to himself and then to the band. "We already started, so I gotta head . . ."

"Sure," I say. "Thanks."

We sit on the floor, and Nze piles a plate with Doritos, garlic bread, and some kind of apple salad. I eat a chip and look around. Everyone's around our age, and they seem into the band: a drummer, singer, guitarist, and Bolt on bass. They finish their song, and, with a mumbled "Thank you, thank you very much!" from the singer, start the next one.

Bolt looks straight at me as familiar notes fill the room. It's Stevie Wonder's "Do I Do," and they don't do a bad job. I take a breath and get my head around being here, inside blue building, two floors below the FGS. It seems like a good time to take the cup of wine Joelle hands me, but it's nasty, so I put it back on the table, lean against the couch, watching Bolt's fingers.

He knows what he's doing on the bass as far as I can tell, and he sounds good singing along on the chorus. I think about when I first met him and he said his own name wrong. Shy, goofy Bolt doesn't seem to be around much anymore. I wonder if I like confident Bolt better.

My heart has been waiting

My soul anticipating . . .

My mind turns to the long day. The view from the ferry. Nze, hungry for Broadway and sex. Joelle's proud expression when she gave the woman the five-dollar bill, even though she's deep in wedding saving.

Five-dollar bills are magic, Mom always taught me. When I was little, money was for saving or paying bills. If I returned a present I'd gotten to the store and the refund was ten dollars or more? Mom would make me put it in the bank, or at least toward an outfit I was saving up for. But a five was for fun. If I helped her download five dollars' worth of coupons, Mom would hand me a crisp bill at the grocery store and tell me it was all mine. We could go to the Dollar Tree or Starbucks.

There was this one time the Dollar Tree had a whole bin of pitch pipes. Uncle Wendell was visiting, and I knew he loved to sing, so I used part of my precious five to buy him one. I'd never seen him giggle like when I gave it to him.

He blew and matched the note with his smooth rich voice until Mom said she had a headache and went for the Tylenol. Uncle Wendell winked at me.

"Your momma never could carry a tune," he whispered. "But you know why I love to sing so much? I wasn't probably but seven years old and my teacher, Ms. Aberworthy, heard me singing to myself during recess. And she said, 'Why, Wendell, if you don't have the prettiest voice.' I remember like it was yester—"

"Wendell!" Mom was back, scowling at Uncle Wendell like he was showing me porn. "We live here now, all right? Clae doesn't need to hear about years ago in the backwoods."

I groan as the song ends in Bolt's friend's dark apartment. That's exactly the problem with Mom. There were ways she was good to Uncle Wendell; always cooked his favorites, sent him birthday presents, bought him clothes so he looked tight, because she thought people would respect him more. And at the same time, she shut

119

him down every chance she got. Just like she does to me, if I want to know about my own family.

Nze taps me. "You two should go."

I nod and tap Joelle, who we decided would go with me because all three of us would be too conspicuous, and Joelle wants to *feel* Grandma/Not Grandma.

We slip into the corridor and walk to the elevator.

"You know what you're gonna say when she answers the door?" Joelle asks.

"Uh . . . ," I say. Not because I haven't thought about it. It's just, the thing I imagine myself saying is literally "I'm Clae." In my mind, that's all it takes. Once I say it, there's melting and hugging and the scene fades to goodness like the end of a Freeform movie.

"Never mind," Joelle says, as the elevator doors open. "You'll be fine."

We step to the side to get our bearings.

Apartment 22 is close enough to see. It has a green doormat. The dark brown door has a peephole. I don't know what happened to the pumped-up girl on the ferry, but the whole thing seems incredibly stupid now. A dog barks in one of the apartments. I swallow.

A door opens down the hall, and my head swivels toward it. A woman comes out of an apartment. She's oldish, Black. Wearing a flower-print skirt and sleeveless blouse. She walks past us. And into number 22.

Joelle grabs my arm. It was her. The FGS.

"Come on!" Joelle says. "This is so cool. She's home!"

I shake my head. She didn't look like she takes a lot of bullshit.

I can't just barge into her house when she just got home. Two days before I'm supposed to meet her!

"Shh!" I tell Joelle. "We have to get out of here!"

"What? But we know she's home."

I've already pushed the button, and the elevator doors open. I jump in like it's a lifeboat.

"You sure?" Joelle asks, as the doors close and I slump against the wall. "I could go feel her door, see what I can tell about her."

"*No!*" I yell. Then, quieter: "We're good." I let out a sound between a groan and a laugh.

"I saw her," I say. "I saw her, and she's real." I'm breathing hard, the image of the FGS dancing in my mind.

"I saw her, and she's real," I say again. And for now, that's enough.

FIFTEEN

IT WAS THE DOG

"What's next on FS Twenty-Five?" I ask Nze, getting to Mr. Barber's room and slipping into my usual spot by the window.

Since the FGS sighting, I've been writing out the list of questions I want to ask her when we finally meet. (*Where is my dad? Why did he leave? What other people are in our family? Why have you been hiding all this time?*) But the meeting's still thirty-two hours away. My strategy to not completely freak out is to keep adding to the list but focus on other things today. I'm planning to pay real attention in class. And since Nze's sleeping over tonight, we can talk about her life, too.

"What?" Nze asks.

"FS Twenty-Five," I tell her. "The *FS* stands for *fun shit.*" I explain the new name I came up with for *her* list. Bucket lists are for old people, and Nze's situation's crap enough without giving it an old-people name. "We can work on whatever's next tonight," I say.

"Thanks, but no thanks?" Nze says. Her face is totally serious. My hand goes to my mouth as I realize it was stupid to make a cute name for her list.

"Nze . . ."

Without a word, she gets up, snatches her bag off the floor, and leaves the room. On the way out, she practically runs into Mr. Barber, who says something jolly.

He eyes me, and even though I'm at the end of the room, calls out, "Too bad Ms. LaSalle had to step out. I have some thoughts for the two of you."

"Uh . . . ," I say, eyes on the spot where Nze disappeared.

Mr. Barber leaves me alone, and Joelle comes in and takes the seat between me and Nze's empty chair. Class starts, but all I can think about is Nze. How could I have been so stupid? She took her bag, so . . . did she leave the building? Is she blowing off our plan for tonight?

Joelle's knee smacks into mine, and I hear Mr. Barber's voice saying, "Ms. Mitchell? Earth calling . . ."

"Sorry," I say. "Yes?"

"I was telling the class that in your original essay, you filled in gaps generally left open in popular renditions of American history, in your case, the Revolutionary War. There are those, however, who argue that journalism deals with current events, not historical ones. I was asking your opinion."

I want to answer, but my brain won't cooperate. He sighs as I blink like a dope.

"Journalism *creates* history," a voice says from across the room. It's Nze, standing in the doorframe. "When you record something that's happening in the present, you're making history for future people, whether you think of it that way or not. So journalists should always go back and look, to see what we left out or got wrong or whatever it is."

Mr. Barber beams at her.

"Yes, gaps! Missing pieces!" Mr. Barber throws up his arms, he's so excited. "Wow me one last time, Ms. LaSalle. What has that to do with *your* original essay?"

"My original essay?" Nze raises her brows, caught out. But she recovers. "Well, it's a thing in disabled communities. People never write about them. And if they do, the articles are about how rotten it is that they get hidden away in institutions and not paid attention to. So nobody knows how much people can actually do, or the choices they have, like schools or technologies they can use. It's like the more they"—she stares right at Mr. Barber—"the more *we* get left out, the more we're gonna be left out."

"Cooking at last!" Mr. Barber says. "Ms. LaSalle, please take your seat. That will take us nicely into our next topic, which is relevant, I believe, to the articles proposed by Mr. Eng and Ms. Roberts . . ."

Nze slips into her seat.

When Mr. Barber looks the other way, I lean over and whisper, "That was so good. You *crushed* it."

"Mm," she says, not even cracking a smile.

"What I said before," I say. "I'm sorry."

"It's not about you," she says, her eyes on Mr. Barber.

The rest of class, I worry that she's not coming over tonight, even though she says her rotten mood's not about me. But I don't ask because I don't want her to say she's not coming.

When our last class ends at five forty-five, Nze's still in her funk. But she acts as though nothing's changed with our plans, just says she wants to get to my neighborhood early and kill the time there before we sneak her into Mrs. Brisbaine's. We end up at the pizza place down the block from Mrs. B's, holed up in the back with my first-ever calzone and a black-and-white cookie each. I try to talk about our project, but she only shrugs or half-assed agrees with whatever I say.

We're almost done eating when she takes a last bite of crispy dough and says, "I can't believe you and Joelle chickened out last night."

"Oh," I say. "It was a lot, seeing her. And I couldn't let her get mad at me for barging in before I even met her. You know?"

The look on Nze's face says she definitely does not know. "I should have gone with you instead of Joelle," she says. "We would've gone in, and it would've been fine."

Really? "Well, I'm gonna see her tomorrow," I say. "So it doesn't really matter." I wrap up my cookie and put it in my bag. "Anyway, thanks for sleeping over. It really helps—"

Nze makes a loud production of crumpling the bag her calzone came in. "You know what I think?" she says. "Probably, this fairy god someone—"

That's it! "Let's just go," I say, gathering up our trash. We're not talking about the FGS while she's being like this.

"It's not too early?" Nze asks.

"We'll take the long way."

Outside, there's a cool breeze. Most of the stores are closed, and some of the streetlights are out. It's dark, and not that many people are on the sidewalks. I lead us in the opposite direction from Mrs. B's, hoping that once around the block will make us late enough so we can finally go in. Then I'll pretend to be tired, and we can just go to bed.

"I really thought about it," Nze says. "And you're better off if mystery whoever *isn't* your grandma, you know. You don't want a grandma who sneaks around and doesn't let her grandkid know who she is." She says it like I've got a bunch of spare grandmas I can go to if this one doesn't work out.

My face burns. "Okay," I say quietly. "You don't have to help me with this. It's not like I asked you to." Sweat breaks out under my arms, but it's too late. I said it, and I'm not taking it back.

"Mm, 'cause you definitely don't need help," Nze says. If she wasn't mad at me before, she is now. She moves to the side, as if she wants to get away from me as much as I want to get away from her. And then, she's down. I stop walking, and it takes a second before I realize she's on the ground, one arm pinned under her body.

"Nze!" I shout, squatting next to her.

She doesn't pop up like most people if they fall, and it freaks me out.

"Nze, are you all right?"

People are gathering. A muscly brown arm cuts in front of my face, and a voice says, "Can I help you up?"

126

Nze finally raises her head. "I'm good," she says, in a raspy voice. "Thanks."

People move away, and Nze shifts so that she's sitting on her butt. I can tell it hurts, but I help her up and we move to the back of the sidewalk. I try to wedge myself under one of her arms, so she can lean on me. She holds up her other hand in a *Keep away* gesture.

"Fuck me, fuck me, fuck me," she says.

"Do you think your arm's broken?" I ask.

Because she looks like it could be. Her shirt's crooked. The hurt arm is scraped to the elbow, and she's holding it at a weird angle.

"It's not that."

"Wait, is one of your legs . . . ?"

"It's 'cause I can't fucking see!" She shouts it, like it's the obvious answer to the world's stupidest question. "That's why I fell. When the light's bad like this . . . everything's one big shadow."

I look around. It's dark, but not so bad that I can't see her face in the glow of a streetlight. It's a new level of intense: embarrassed and hurt and sad. Tears sparkle in her eyes.

"We just need to take you to Mrs. B's," I say. "We'll say you were going home, but you got hurt and her place was closer. That way, if we need help . . ."

Nze shakes her head. "I don't want to talk to anybody else. I can wait, let's just get out of here."

I lead her back toward Mrs. B's. The porch light's on when we get there, and I guide her to the little nook between the staircase rail and Mrs. B's rosebushes.

"Do you want to try to sit down?" I ask, even though the only place to sit is the patch of concrete that Mrs. B calls her yard.

Nze shakes her head. "That sucked so hard," she says quietly.

"Has it . . . Does it happen a lot?" I ask.

"It happens," she says.

She stares at the street, and I can't think of anything to say. When it's time to go in, things go according to plan. Mrs. B's already in bed and doesn't want to talk any more than I do. I put my bag down in my room, then creep back out and listen by her door until I can hear her snoring. Then, I go back for Nze.

When I'm alone in the bathroom, Nze in my room in her pj's, I remember we were fighting before she fell. It feels like that was a hundred years ago. And the meeting with Grandma/Not Grandma feels a hundred years in the future. I keep seeing Nze's face, staring at the street under the porch light.

I wander back down the hall and open my door. She's sitting on my bed, legs crisscrossed and head back, putting eye drops in her eyes. When she's done, she squeezes her eyes shut, I guess to keep the drops in.

"I want to tell you what it's like," she says. "I never told anybody, except my mom."

"Okay," I say, climbing on the bed to sit across from her. She opens her eyes and keeps going.

"People think it's like being nearsighted, which I've been all my life. If you're nearsighted, you can see things, even if they're too far away, or too small to get into focus. But this bitch glaucoma . . . it's about *darkness*. Darkness that creeps in from the edges till you can only see a little patch in front of you. And there's a kind of veil over that, like you're looking through something dark and gauzy."

"It's like that even in the daytime?" I ask. I don't want to be nosy. But Mom always says about her patients, if someone's going through something you don't understand, it's best to ask.

"You don't notice the black around the edges so much when it's light out. Especially in the eye that's better." She touches her left eye. "And the gauzy part isn't as dark. But it's not like before. It's hard to even remember how bright things used to seem in the daytime."

"Wow . . ."

"That's not what I really wanted to tell you," Nze says. "I want to tell you what happened this morning." She pushes back against my pillows and hugs her knees.

"It was the dog," she says.

"You've got a *dog*?"

"I *need* a dog. Sapphire Simone. My guide dog. I've known what her name will be ever since I found out about the disease. I got her collar online, big-ass fake jewels. We were going to be divas together." She sniffs. "Anyhoo . . . I sent my eye test results to the dog people. This morning, they got back to me. They said I'm not blind enough to get my dog. Can you believe that? I'm not blind enough for the one thing that might make me be able to stand this, but I'm too blind to not fall on my face."

The tears are back, sadness in liquid form, pooled at the edges of her eyes. I wish I could draw how she looks, feeling so much and letting it show.

"Is it just . . . can you only go to that one place?"

"They're the ones that have all German shepherds," she says. "And it gets worse. Even if I were blind enough—even when I am—I have to learn to walk with a cane first, so I don't"—she does air quotes—"*over-rely on the dog.* And after all that, once I'm blind enough and I can use the stupid cane, it can still take a *year* to get my dog!"

"Sapphire," I say, because I'm already picturing the two of them together.

We go quiet. After a while, I climb under the covers, and Nze does, too.

"*You* talk," she says. "You're the one with the big day tomorrow."

But I don't want to. Even though the way Nze is now, sad and open and real, she seems like the easiest person in the world to talk to. I just don't want to talk about me or the FGS. Nze has me out of my head, and it feels good.

"No, you," I say. "About anything."

She waits a couple of beats. "Was I a huge bitch tonight?" she asks. "I guess I don't get your thing. I've known everything about my family forever. But maybe that's because a kind of big thing was part of our history."

"Yeah?"

"On my dad's side," Nze says. "It's a weird story. Wanna hear?"

I'm staring at the ceiling, which has shadows from the street-lights outside. I don't think I can really hear Mrs. B's breathing or the refrigerator humming, but for the first time, I imagine them. Peaceful nighttime sounds.

"Yup," I say, not even blinking at the ceiling. "I wanna hear."

"It starts with my grandpa, my dad's dad, whose name was Sonny. Sonny grew up in Virginia, and he was the first one in our family to go to college and get a job that wasn't farming."

Virginia. My mind jumps to Uncle Wendell.

"People talk about him in our family," Nze says, "because he did all that even though *his* dad was wrecked. He—Sonny's dad—had been in World War Two and he'd ended up in a Nazi camp for a while. Afterward he could never really sleep, and it made it so he couldn't keep a job or anything."

"But he had enough money to send his kid to college?" I ask.

"His wife, my great-grandma, worked as a maid—they call it a domestic—and she sewed really beautiful dresses and quilts that she sold. They made it work. But that's not the point of the story. The point is, Grandpa Sonny grew up hearing these stories about the war and the concentration camps—not like details, his dad, Great-Grandpa Montrose, never gave details, but Sonny knew it happened, and he thought it was super noble, you know? Going overseas to save these people from these camps. Even though he ended up in one himself for a while, he was part of the liberation, of bringing it all down and making it so the Nazis weren't in power anymore. So, when Grandpa Sonny got old, and Great-Grandpa Montrose was way old, Sonny found out about this thing where American soldiers who had ended up in camps could get money from the German government. Reparations, like the Jewish people got for all the shit they went through. And he did all this paperwork, worked his ass off, my grandpa, and he actually got it for his dad."

"Wow. I never learned anything like that when we did World War Two."

"Me either. And that money made all the difference. Grandpa Sonny had gone to college, but he still didn't have a lot. But when he got the reparations, he and his dad decided it would be our family nest egg. It would be our backup for if there was trouble or some big opportunity. My dad used some of it to buy our house. And it's why I'd be able to go to that German eye clinic if I wanted."

"That's . . . amazing," I say. We lie quietly a long time. My mind goes from Nazi Germany to Mom and Uncle Wendell and all the things that could be possible in our family history.

I think I've been asleep when Nze's voice calls me back.

"Can you imagine?" she says. "I could get a cane for my eighteenth birthday."

I open my eyes, keep them on the shadowy ceiling.

"Here's the thing," she says. "I don't think I can do that out here alone. I may have to go back to my parents."

There's silence and then a sniff. I turn to look at her. And, finally, her tears spill.

SIXTEEN

THE FGS

"*This* place?" I ask, looking at the restaurant. Through the glass walls, you can see why it's called the Checkerboard Bistro. The floor's made of black and white tiles, the walls are white with thick black trim, and the tables are black with white chairs.

"It's L-shaped," Nze says, pointing to the end of the block where the restaurant rounds the corner onto the side street. "I can be on one end, Joelle on the other, you in the middle, so we can see what goes on."

"We can all sit together first, though, right?" I ask. We have a half hour before the FGS gets here, and I'm a mess of excitement and stress.

We head inside, where it's even weirder than it looked from the street. The L shape makes you dizzy with all the black and white. The servers have on black jackets and white aprons, adding moving parts to the whole mess.

"I forgot to tell you," Joelle says, leading us to a table in the middle of the L. "Chaz is coming here, too. But never mind that now. I have news. My sister found out about the wedding!"

"Oh shit. She told your parents?" I ask. I don't want to be talking about anything but the FGS, but this is real, too—I know how bad she wanted to keep her secret.

"Well, no," she says.

"Then . . . ?"

"Now she wants in on everything!" Joelle says. "She's like a nightmare, my little sister, she'll try to take over with her stupid ideas and even worse taste. I had to tell her I already had a dress, and then I made the three of us an appointment for later at this place I want to get it from. Please say you can make it! That's the other reason Chaz is coming here. I can't see him tonight since we'll be dress shopping, and—"

"God forbid you miss a night of each other," Nze fills in.

"Exactly!" Joelle squeals "So can you come, after?"

I look at Nze to see how she feels about another night out, after she fell last night. But she says she can make it.

"Wait till you meet my sister at the wedding," Joelle says. "She's like an anime villain, all giant eyes and look-at-me energy. I honestly think she's whitemailing me, in this creepy weird way."

"She's what?" I ask.

"You know, instead of blackmail, whitemail—since enough already with all the bad stuff being black. What I mean is, my sister's gonna make me let her in all my wedding stuff or else she'll tell my mom. Is that not the worst?"

I wonder what it would be like to have a sister you don't like.

But I don't ask because the door opens, and a Black woman walks in. My heart shuts down. I'm sure it's her. Then she turns, and I see that it's not the same woman from 2200 Flatlands. But not before my heart started up again, triple tempo against my chest.

"It's time," I say. "You gotta go so I can get ready."

"Oh," Joelle says, sounding disappointed. "Okay."

They both get up and, each squeezing one of my arms, disappear to their "stations." I watch Nze a sec, half wanting to call her back. Then I pour some water from the bottle on the table to help my dry mouth and take my folding mirror out of my bag. The yellow dress Mom got me from the secondhand store looks stupid against all the black and white. It seemed grandma-ish when I finally decided this morning, but now it looks like I'm trying to be Black Alice in Wonderland. I groan, close the mirror, and look at my phone. Seven minutes. There's jazz music playing, so I close my eyes and listen a minute, feeling the jitters burning in my stomach, chest, and throat. And then there's a voice.

"Are you Clae?"

I look up, not too freaked because it's a guy's voice, so it can't be her. He's standing behind the seat across the table. "Clae Mitchell? I'm Angus Williston, Mrs. Taylor Rose's personal assistant."

"You're . . . ?"

"Here for Mrs. Taylor Rose," he says. "She asked me to come and meet you."

Slowly, it sinks in that he's talking about the FGS. *Mrs. Taylor Rose?*

"Where is she?" I ask, looking around for the woman in the flowered skirt.

"She won't be able to make it," he says.

"She . . ."

"I can explain." He pulls out the chair and sits. I notice his dark brown skin and suck-up smile as thick tears well in my throat and spring to the back of my eyes. I swallow them back, because I'm not giving them to this guy, whoever he is. I pull out my phone and text Nze and Joelle.

Me: She's not coming. She sent this guy. Let's go.

Nze texts back first.

Nze: Nah, roll with it. You never know.

The guy, Angus, picks up the QR code from the table, scans it with his phone like we just came here to eat, and says, "Yaaas, a club and fries. Perfect. You want to see?" He offers his phone. When I don't take it, he shrugs. "It's all on Mrs. Taylor Rose, so we might as well enjoy."

My fingers start to pick at each other. A server comes over and asks for our drink orders, and Angus asks for a maple French toast latte, then adds, "Make it two," when I don't order.

All I can think is, *I'm not going to meet her.*

"Why didn't she come?" I ask when the server's gone. "Like she said she would."

"Jumping right in, then," Angus says. "Well. She said I could give you her card, to start us off." He takes one from his pocket and hands it across the table. It reads:

R. Taylor Rose

Seven Founts Foundation

Caring. Sharing. Daring.

It's got a little logo of a fountain with seven spouts shooting into a sunrise. There's an email that has the foundation's name in it, but no phone number.

"So?" I say.

"Mrs. Taylor Rose wants you to know the nature of her . . . gosh . . . *her help* to you, over the years. She's a member of Seven Founts, a private foundation that helps promising Black girls realize their potential. She and her establishment have been your anonymous benefactors," he says.

"I don't understand," I say, even though it's not true. I know what an anonymous benefactor is. But the thought of the FGS being an *anonymous benefactor . . . a stranger whose whole point is to stay a stranger*? Ice-cold stones drop in my belly.

"It's like you won the lottery!" Angus says, grinning. "You just didn't know it. And I hope you know how honored you should be, the foundation only picks a few girls each year. . . ."

The foundation. I take a breath. Turning away from Angus so I can think, I go over it in my head. The bank deposits on Mom's screen, the box hidden in the back of her closet, the unaffordable presents. Okay, it fits, but . . . I pick up my phone and google *R. Taylor Rose*. Nothing. I try *Seven Founts Foundation*. Zip. Right. That's why it's anonymous.

"So if it's a big secret," I say to Angus, "how come you're telling me?"

"The information you're getting now is un-prec-e-dent-ed," he says, tapping the table with every syllable. "Mrs. Taylor Rose wanted me to tell you that. But because you were so persistent"—he holds up a hand to the side of his mouth and says in a high voice—"*pushy* . . . well, she decided to make an exception." He laughs at his joke.

I shake my head against a new wave of hurt. She's not coming, and she sent this guy only because I was being pushy. *She's not family.*

"What about my mom?" I ask, my mind bouncing back to the bank transfers. "All this time, she's been getting money?"

"Parents get less information than you'd think," Angus says. "Just that their kids were chosen. Most parents don't ask a lot of questions. We promise that once the girls reach adulthood and get going in their careers, the foundation will tell them everything."

"And they're supposed to just wait?"

"Yup," Angus says.

I try to picture Mom sitting on this for years and years and not telling me. Every A paper or good test score I ever got was taped to the door, my worst art framed on the living room wall. How would she stand not telling me I got *chosen*?

The server shows up with our drinks. My sip takes me right back to Mom, who'd kill for it. Just like she'd die to tell me something like this. Across the table, Angus is grooving on his drink. I look him hard in his eyes, the color of coffee beans. Something's not right, here. Right?

"I want to meet her," I say. "I want to meet R. Taylor Rose."

He freezes with the cup still touching his lips, then slowly lowers it. "That's not a choice we have," he says.

"Then why'd you come here? What's the point, if she doesn't want to meet me?"

"Finally!" he says. "A question I can answer!" Happy again, he picks up his leather backpack, takes out a flat box, and lays it on the table. With a stupid little hand flourish, he opens the box. "I have been authorized to offer you an *enhanced Seven Founts experience.* Mrs. Taylor Rose is trying to convince her colleagues to add something new to their package. You'd be our lucky little guinea pig."

"*Guinea pig?*"

"In such a good way!"

"So, this is more foundation stuff?"

"What do you mean?" he says. "Of course it's foundation stuff. Usually the support ends with high school, but Mrs. Taylor Rose thinks a lot of girls need a few more focused experiences to succeed in their best lives. She'd like to give you those experiences while you're in New York. And the best part is"—he flashes me a smarmy smile—"I get to go with you!"

My eyes narrow. Is he messing with me? But he just sits there, waiting for me to get excited. When I don't, he goes on.

"I'm talking upscale restaurants, concerts, the hottest tickets on Broadway. *We can do those things while you're here.*" He says it like I'm a little slow.

I stand. Give up.

"I gotta go," I say. "If she doesn't want to meet me . . ."

I scan for Nze and Joelle. They're both looking at me, and I realize for the first time that Chaz is with Joelle now, and they're just one table away. Nze's by the door we came in, but I like the idea of turning my back on Angus and using the door behind me.

"Tell Mrs. Whoever I don't need more stuff from her," I say.

"I'll follow up!" Angus calls after me as I head across the checkered floor.

A second later, I'm out the door. The fresh air and bright sun hit me like I've been in a cave for a century. I walk to the next building, so I can't be seen through the Checkerboard Bistro's glass walls, and bend over, hands to knees, breathing heavy. *Angus? The Seven Founts Foundation?* Nothing that just happened makes sense to me.

"What in hell was that about?" Nze asks, coming up beside me and looking over her shoulder.

"I don't even . . . ," I start. "She . . . I don't want to talk about it. Not yet."

Both our phones buzz. Nze checks. "Joelle wants us to meet her near her dress place, she has something to do first. She's sending the address."

She types a response, then says, "Come on, let's get out of here."

Even though Angus just blew up my world, I haven't forgotten that Nze could fall again. I slip my arm in hers, pretending like I need support—not that I don't—so I can hold on to her.

"You don't want to tell any of it?" she asks.

I fish the card out of my dress pocket and, instead of handing it to her, read it out loud. "'R. Taylor Rose,'" I read. "'The Seven Founts Foundation.' That's who's supposed to be the FGS."

"So, not somebody in your family?"

"Mmm."

"Then, who was that guy?"

"Her assistant, I guess?"

"Who you blew off. At least from how it looked."

Tears threaten again as I remember seeing Angus standing there, and realize there wasn't going to be a Grandma/Not Grandma. I give another "Mmm," and Nze does a good job not asking for more. Eventually, she leads us into a café—a nice regular one, the kind that could be in Gloucester. We sit down and order fries. I cross my arms on the table and put my head down. I *saw* her at 2200 Flatlands. I thought she was my grandma, or maybe my aunt.

What if I had knocked that night? Would she have even opened the door?

"Listen," Nze says. "Just because you didn't meet them today, it doesn't mean your family doesn't exist."

"What?"

"Whatever happened with that guy, back there," she says, "it's got nothing to do with what you told us about your uncle—him telling you you're not alone, giving you the ring like it was gonna lead you to your dad or something. I'm just saying, all that's still the same. It's got nothing to do with what happened today."

A server brings the fries. I stare at them and let what Nze said sink in. Uncle Wendell and the ring. J. M. Smith High School. Even if the money and the presents came from this stupid foundation . . . there could still be whatever Uncle Wendell was leading me to . . . which could be a way to find my dad's family. Somehow, I'd never really separated Uncle Wendell's "evidence" from the rest.

"I guess that's real," I say, feeling a little better. "So, I should think of the ring as my main evidence now and try to forget about the money and the presents and Whoever Taylor Rose?"

Nze nods encouragement. Then, someone steps to our table and we look up. It's Joelle, with Chaz right behind her.

"I thought he wasn't coming," Nze says. "Because of the dress thing."

"He wasn't," Joelle says. She squats down between our chairs. "*Until* we found out some things. That's why we hung back, to make absolutely sure." She and Chaz trade a look that's smug, even for them.

"Can you just tell us what's going on?" I ask, not in the mood for games.

Joelle pulls Chaz closer, stroking his hand like it's made of mink. "Well, we overheard everything," she says. "And Chaz, my Chaz, right here? He knows how to find Mrs. R. Taylor Rose."

SEVENTEEN

THE STORY THRIFTIQUE

"It gets better," Joelle says. "Tell them, baby."

Chaz pulls chairs from another table, and we all crowd around our little two-top, the three of us turned to him. He's all grins.

"I don't *know them, know them*," he says. "But my mom's big in philanthropy, and she's talked about the whole shadow field—you know, the anonymous people who never go public. They still do stuff with each other, though, and my mom, she's not one of them, but she likes to host things. I've seen papers at the house after she's had people in. I remembered that Seven Founts logo." He slides his hand out of Joelle's and drops it over her shoulders, scooching his chair even closer. "Seven's my lucky number, since we met on July seventh."

"So?" I ask, needing him to get to it already.

"I can ask my mom and see what she knows about that woman," Chaz says.

He's excited to help, but it doesn't do anything to change the bad feeling in my stomach. And it adds to the confusion fuzzing up my brain. If Chaz can find R. Taylor Rose, is there any chance he'd be finding Grandma/Not Grandma? No, right? Just some philanthropy lady, which would make me feel like crap all over again.

"So, your family's loaded?" Nze says to Chaz. Because Joelle said . . ."

Chaz looks startled. "I don't know about loaded," he says. "They're comfortable, partly because they're cheap as hell. They believe in saving and giving, not so much spending. Doesn't matter to us, though, Joelle and me are doing our own thing. Right, babe?"

"Right," Joelle says. "Chaz has a job instead of college, and I do temp stuff. And his family supports us *emotionally*. They know about the wedding."

There's a pause where I guess everybody thinks about that— Chaz's supportive rich family that's not paying for the wedding.

Then Joelle throws her arms up in a big gesture and says, "Anywayyyy! It sounds like that guy Angus got sent by this R. Taylor Rose person, right? But she's staying behind the scenes for whatever reason. So how cool is it that Chaz might know how to get to her?"

Chaz holds his hands up for a high five. I don't meet them, but Nze does it for me.

"Very cool," she says. "But let's say we figure all that out later? Aren't we supposed to be dress shopping now?"

Joelle squeals. Nze and I share the rest of the fries with Joelle and Chaz, and in a few minutes, we all get up to go. It feels good to be out in the sunshine. The streets are narrow, lined with shops, and full of young people in good clothes. Chaz takes off. As the three of us walk on, I remind myself I've never shopped for a wedding dress before. I should get into it—forget the FGS, at least for a while.

"And . . . ta-da!" Joelle throws out her free arm toward a narrow storefront. The sign above it reads *True Story: A Bridal Thriftique* in old-fashioned writing. In the window, gold light glints off a satiny white dress, with a bow tie, garter, and dressy shoes arranged all around it. Right off, I can tell it's the kind of thrift shop that makes shopping nice for their customers, not the kind that makes you paw through piles of whatever to find what you need and the staff acts like they're not supposed to help since you're getting stuff cheap.

"It's appointments only," Joelle says. "So we get the whole place for just us. And here's the best part. See those pieces of paper?" She points to printed pages clipped on silver wire at the back of the window. "Those are the stories. The way it works is you pick your dress by the story that goes with it. Like if the bride and groom were star-crossed lovers, or friends since kindergarten, or met in a bathroom and got married on a yacht. And we match *our* story—like mine and Chaz's—to the dresses' stories, till we find the perfect match."

"Wait . . . ," I say, trying to get my head around it.

Nze's ahead of me.

"So," she says. "Let's see. You're supposed to find another teen bride getting interracial-married on the down-low to a seems-like-he's-rich-after-all white guy from Jersey?"

"Oh, ha," Joelle says. "It's about falling *in love* with the story because it speaks to you. So you feel connected to, like, this essential meta story when you wear the dress."

Meta story? This time I almost laugh, except that Joelle looks too sincere. I'm grateful, honestly, for something this weird to take my mind off what just happened.

"Come on!" Joelle runs up the stairs and rings the bell. A woman answers.

"Oh," she says, looking us over. "You're younger than I thought." She shrugs. "Well, you'll decide what works. Who's the bride?"

"That'd be me!" Joelle bends her knees and wiggles her whole body.

"Lead the way," the woman says. She ushers us into a dark hallway and through another door at the back end.

Sunlight hits us when she opens it. We're in a medium-size room with windows at the back and a million silver wires like the ones we saw in the window, hanging from the ceiling. All of them have printed cream-colored cards clipped to the end, and they're staggered at different lengths. There are two tables along the walls with jewelry, shoes, and little bags. And there's a puffy velvet cream-colored couch with a coffee table in front, where there's fancy glasses and a bottle sticking out of a bucket. The whole place isn't much bigger than Mrs. Brisbaine's TV room, and the silvery wire and velvety couches make it feel like a rich person's bedroom, more than anything. Joelle looks around, dazed.

"Where are the dresses?" she asks.

"Dresses?" The woman sticks a finger on her chin, fake thinking about it. Now that I get a better look at her, I see she's light brown-skinned and has on a pale blue sleeveless dress. Middle Eastern? Latinx? Her bare, muscled arms shoo us toward the couch.

"Sit, please. If anyone wants soda water instead of champagne,

I can get you some. Whatever you choose, when you pick up your drink, you leave whatever's on your mind behind."

I get a lump in my throat. I still feel like my grandma just died and took my whole family with her.

"We're agreed, then?" the Thriftique woman asks in her no-nonsense manner. Her big brown eyes soft, but firm. "My name is Lina," she says. "And you're correct, no dresses. That's why we're the True Story Thriftique, not the Dressbarn. And, trust me, I have nothing against the Dressbarn. But here, it's all about the story." She points to the cards clipped to the silver wires. "Once you've picked five stories, I'll go back to the storeroom to get their matching dresses."

"Now, bride?" she says to Joelle. "Tell your friends the top three things they should know about your love with"—she checks a card in her hand—"*Chaz,* in order to help you pick out a story. Don't overthink it, just boom-boom-boom, top three things about you and Chaz."

Joelle looks nervous, but she nods, closes her eyes, and says, "*One*—he loves me. I didn't ever get what that would feel like when I was little, and I would dream about it. And it feels so amazing, to know for sure. *Two,* the interracial thing. We know it's real and it can get hard sometimes. But we can handle it, because we're us. And *three . . .*" She looks up from under her lashes, a tiny smile on her lips. "I'm sure the other way, too. That I love him. And that's really not gonna change. I wouldn't take a chance, getting married so young, if I weren't sure."

"Perfect!" Lina says. "Now, go find your story—the one that says Joelle and Chaz are part of this tradition, they belong here!

You can unclip the ones you like, then come back to the couch to compare notes. Yes?"

"Yaaas!" Joelle jumps up and dives in.

Nze follows her. I take a sip of the champagne, which I've had before at Mom's coworker's wedding. It tastes . . . dry and sour, but I feel it right away, making my head swim, and my thoughts seem far away. I take a big gulp. I really want to be here for Joelle, not stuck in my own stuff.

"Five at a time," Lina reminds us, "but you'll want to go through a lot of stories before you pick your five."

I pick a silver wire and check out the card. It's the kind of card that opens, so that what I'm looking at is the cover, which has just one word printed on it. It reads, *Wild*. Looking around, all the cards are like that—just a few words on the outside. There's *Perfection*, *Double Trouble*, *Over-the-Top*, *Courageous*, *Cozy*, *Defiant*, *About the Friends*. On my other side, there's one that just has a dollar sign. Another reads *Free*, and one reads *Unexpected*. I start with that one, because what isn't unexpected about Joelle and Chaz? When I flip the cover up, there's handwriting in pen, neat and pretty:

> *I planned my wedding on the side of a mountain, where everyone could see down on a winding river. That morning, my uncle decided we needed binoculars to enjoy the view. He held up the whole ceremony and went to get them, but then everyone was mad at him, so he got nervous and pitched a pair of binoculars off the side of the mountain. My aunt thought it was a person who fell and had a panic attack. By the time she calmed*

down, the minister had to go. We ended up getting married in the backyard of our Airbnb, by a justice of the peace. It was beautiful. My aunt wept happy tears the whole time.

BIG TAKEAWAY: EMBRACE THE UNEXPECTED!

That one would be better for Nze than Joelle, I think, going on to *Free*, which is all about a gay couple whose families danced barefoot together at their wedding.

"Question," Nze asks, coming over with an empty glass. "With the champagne and getting the whole place to ourselves like this? How much do you think these dresses cost?"

"From fifty bucks," Lina says, not even pretending she wasn't eavesdropping. "To over a hundred grand. It all depends."

"On . . . ?" Nze asks. "Because it can't depend on the story."

"Depending on the dress. But if your friend finds the right one, she could pay me fifty bucks and go home as happy as the bride who paid fifty times as much."

"But you won't know till you try on the dress?"

"That's correct."

"So, what if you fall for a dress that costs a hundred grand, and you don't have a hundred grand?"

"We have payment plans," Lina says. "But, ladies, please. Trust. Don't worry about problems that aren't happening."

Nze throws Lina a shady look and goes back to reading story cards. I think about what she said. *Trust.* Ha! How am I supposed to trust anyone when no one will tell me anything? When people talk in riddles and don't show up when they promised to? And what am I supposed to do with this curveball, this Angus?

I'm starting to spiral out when Joelle lets out a gasp. She's holding a card so we can see the outside. It reads, *Gamble*. The writing on the inside is big and loopy:

No, ma'am, we didn't get married in Vegas. We got married at city hall with our two best friends for witnesses. We met in a weekend workshop on financial planning, and we fell in love over the next week. It was so mind-blowing, earth-shaking, body-quaking that we decided to get married to show each other that we weren't dreaming. It didn't feel like a gamble at the time. Now, though, when I look back? I see it was. That was twenty-six years ago and we are just as happy.

BIG TAKEAWAY: TRUST YOUR GUT AND GAMBLE ON LOVE.

"I'm pretty sure this is it," Joelle says.

"I still insist you choose five," Lina says. "It's part of our process, you need to see a progression to know which dress is the correct one for you."

"Well, I kind of like this one." She holds up a card that reads, *Perfect Imperfection*. "What about you two?" She looks from me to Nze.

"I liked *Free*," I tell her.

"I took *Over-the-Top*, and *All About Love*," Nze says.

"Great, so that's five." Joelle gathers the cards and hands them to Lina, who looks like she thinks we're cheating by doing it so fast. But she points Nze and me back to the couch and disappears through a side door, telling Joelle to follow.

Nze and I drink more champagne.

"I know that was rough," Nze says. "Back at the café. Remember what I said, though, it's not over. And we're going to the library soon, and we can dig into that high school your dad went to. Okay?"

"'Course it's not okay," I say. "But yeah. I should focus on the ring and the school."

"Good," she says, picking up my glass and handing it to me. "Do you think I should try to find a wedding outfit while I can still see it? It's not on the list."

"You're sure you want to get married?" I ask.

"Not you?" she says.

"No, I do. I just can't really picture it yet."

"Me either," Nze says, shrugging.

I look around at the promises literally hanging off the ceiling. Maybe it's because such a shitty deal went down with my parents that I can't picture a forever situation. But the champagne's making me feel slow and sleepy, so who knows. I rest my head on the back of the couch. There's a gasp from some other room.

"Joelle?" Nze calls.

"It's the best, seeing myself in a wedding gown!" Joelle calls out to us. "You ready?"

I sit up as we say we are. Out Joelle comes, wrapped in white lace, toga style, with a border of green leaves across the top, and a long lacy veil.

"Wow," I say.

"I know," Joelle says. "Lina says we have to go in reverse order, least-best story to best-best. It's pretty, but I don't think this one's it." She does a last twirl in the mirror and hurries back to the dressing room.

Next comes a silky cream-colored jumpsuit with a crazy-long train, a gauzy three-quarter-length dress, then a skimpy lace one that my mom would say looks like underwear. It's fun enough to pull me out of my head awhile, but I'm drifting back to the *that was so not Grandma* fiasco when Joelle whispers from behind the dressing room door.

"Wait till you see!" she says, sounding so excited she's out of breath.

I shake off Angus and drink some water that Lina brought out.

The dress is bright white silk, bare at the shoulders and wrapped in tight diagonal layers around her body, ending in a slant cut toward the tops of her long thighs. On her head is a short silky veil attached to a frilly cap that makes you think of a backward baseball cap. It's like somebody made a Joelle bride doll and brought it to life.

"It's perfect," Nze says, standing up to admire it. "That's *Gamble*?"

"It is," Joelle says, turning to look at her butt. Even if I hated the dress, I'd know it was perfect from how happy Joelle looks wearing it.

"If my opinion counts," Lina says, "it's unanimous. I've never seen a more perfect fit. I'm not sure there's anything to alter even."

"Wait!" I say, remembering what Mom always says about trying on stuff that might be uncomfortable once you get it out of the store. "Sit down in it, see how it does."

Joelle sits on the couch with us, and the dress still looks perfect.

"It's actually made to go from table to dance floor without any fuss," Lina says. "It's really a thoughtfully designed garment."

"Does thoughtfully designed mean mad expensive?" Nze says.

Joelle's giant smile fades. "I guess it's time to ask," she says. "How much is it?"

Lina purses her lips. "You did select one of our pricier gowns, but by no means the most expensive. And, of course, I can reduce the price a bit if you don't need alterations."

"Yeah, okay," Joelle says, her tongue poking out of her mouth now as she braces herself.

"So, in that case," Lina says, smiling, "the cost will be eight thousand dollars."

"For a used wedding dress?" Nze says.

"For a dress whose story speaks to her," Lina says. "Be honest, Joelle. Would you have picked that dress if it was just hanging off a rack?"

Joelle shakes her head. "I thought I wanted to go full-length," she says.

Lina looks smug.

"Half the fun's in looking, anyway," I say. "We've still got time."

"It's payable in installments," Lina says, ignoring me. "But we do need a deposit of twenty-five percent."

"Wow," Joelle says softly. "That's exactly how much we budgeted for the whole thing. Two thousand dollars. I thought it was so much." She stands up and makes her way out from behind the coffee table. "I'd better take it off," she says.

When she's gone, Lina offers us more champagne and pours it into our glasses without waiting for an answer. I leave my glass where it is. A minute later, Joelle comes out with the dress on a hanger.

"We'll find something else," Nze says, as both of us stand up.

"There have to be other thrift shops," I say, thinking we just need a less snooty one.

"We're taking it," Joelle says, her voice kind of breathless. "I'm gambling on us. That's the whole point, right? And what's eight thousand dollars compared to a lifetime of love?"

"Look," Nze says. "That first one you tried was gorgeous, how much is that?" She looks at Lina, who looks at Joelle.

"Do you want to know?"

Joelle shakes her head. "This is my dress. We'll find the money." She reaches in her bag and pulls out a rolled-up wad of bills.

"Is that two grand in cash?" Nze asks.

"It's Chaz's savings. Not from his parents, from his jobs. We got it out of the bank this morning."

"So, how much is left in there?" I ask, hoping maybe they've got something close to the eight they need.

"Three hundred and seventy-four dollars," she says. "How long do we have to pay?" she asks Lina.

"We'll just need your final payment by the day of your wedding. Deposits are nonrefundable, of course, since we'll have taken the dress off the floor. Only fair."

Nze says, "I don't think so!" and I say, "Joelle!" at the same time. But Joelle pushes the roll of bills into Lina's hands.

"And don't think we're gonna ask Chaz's parents for it, either," she says to us. "We'd never do that, and they wouldn't give it to us if we did."

"Then what the hell's the plan?" Nze asks.

"Why do you think they call it gambling?" Joelle says. And she walks out the door.

EIGHTEEN

WINS

"You thinking about the FGS again?" Nze asks.

We're in my bruised-banana yellow room, me at my desk, Nze on my bed, both lost in our own heads. Mr. Barber's given us a Handle Your Business Day. Classes are canceled and we're supposed to take the day to deep dive into our projects—researching, writing, or getting help from him—whatever it takes to get to the next level.

Nze, Joelle, and I really need the day. In the last five days, Nze's had three doctor's appointments, Joelle's thought up ten get-rich-quick schemes, and I've tried not to think about the nightmare at the checkerboard café. And for once, after a long Brisbaine breakfast with Nze, that part's working.

"I'm thinking about Zach," I tell her. And roll my eyes at the smile that comes on my own face. I can't help it. I miss the beach and I miss Zach, and having a whole day next weekend just to hang by the water again? It feels like exactly what I need after all that's happened in New York.

"Does that mean bad news for Bolt the bass guy?"

"I haven't even kissed Bolt yet," I say.

"Do you want to?"

It's not like I haven't thought of it. "I mean, yeah," I say. "But it'd be weird kissing him when I know I'm gonna be kissing Zach again." I consider for a second, then, because it's Nze, just say what I'm thinking. "They smell really different."

"I know what you mean," she says. "Smells make you feel really close to a person. So, if you're close in the same way to two different people-smells . . . that other person's smell would always be in your head."

"*That!*" I say, with a laugh. "What about you? Any closer to checking *sex, sex, sex* off your list?"

Nze waits a beat. "I know I get loud about it," she says. "But it's hard to think about when I'm so . . . when every day's so all about my vision." Sad Nze creeps up in her eyes.

"We better get to it, huh?" I say. "We have to review everything before the library this afternoon."

Nze picks up her laptop from beside her on the bed. I mentally cross my fingers. It's not even just that I don't want her to be sad. We're behind on our project and need to keep our grades up. Plus, now that I'm trying to let go of 2200 Flatlands and focus on my dad's high school ring, the research we're doing for the project is my best shot at getting information.

"I'll read the pitch," Nze says. "And we can go from there."

Nze reads. "'Black Learning on the Down-Low: Why the Move to Erase Black History in Education Is Dangerous but Doomed.'" She looks up. "I still like our title."

"Read the rest," I say.

"'This article will explore Black independent education over many years,'" Nze reads. "'Including Freedom Schools, which were founded in the 1960s because public education taught inaccurate Black history. These Freedom Schools are original forms of modern homeschooling and have their roots in the first *African* Freedom Schools, established before the Civil War. Even back then, parents and students took leadership to get the best possible curriculum and learning experience. This article will include interviews, research, and analysis to shed light on this ignored but important piece of American history that is relevant to today's struggles against the anti-woke education movement.'"

"Not bad," I say. "And, so far, we know a bunch about this guy, James McCune Smith, who they named my dad's school after." I shuffle through the note cards I've made. "We know he was a superstar at the Mulberry School, the African Freedom School he went to, back in the 1800s. And we have good stuff from the Freedom School movement in the 1960s.

"The problem is, we need more about what was happening in my dad's time, like around the 2000s, to find out how it all fits together. Not to mention, for me to find out more about my dad."

"That's what we'll get at the Schomburg," Nze says. "We'll look for original records from your dad's school, and curriculum from other Freedom Schools." She types into our doc as she talks. "And we'll get more on that school for Black blind kids way back in nineteen-whatever. And other schools around the country."

"And Joelle's gonna do"—I do air quotes—"*Black elite schools.*"

"Yup. Let's call her"—Nze's finger hovers over her phone—"and make sure she's getting back from Atlantic City in time to meet us. I still can't believe they went there."

She hits Joelle's number and puts her phone on speaker. A few seconds later we hear clanging bells. Then Joelle's voice, shouting.

"Quick! I need a number from each of you!"

"You need a what?" Nze asks.

"A number between double zero and thirty-six."

Chaz's voice comes in from farther away. "I think we should just bet red or black, babe."

And Joelle says, "Shush, I got this!"

A serious *dingdingdingdingding* starts up in the background. I picture the whole scene, Joelle and Chaz on red stools, the casino guy in a suit and tie waiting for their numbers before they spin the big wheel.

"You should've left there by now," Nze complains.

But Joelle shouts over her, "Come on! Give me the numbers!"

"Seven!" I yell from the bed, because if she's doing it, I don't want her to miss her chance.

"Fine," Nze says. "Thirty-two. But—"

"Great, call you back!" Joelle hangs up, and Nze and I stare at the phone.

"Do you think they bet their whole three hundred and seventy-four dollars on this?" I ask.

"I can't even," Nze says.

*　　*　　*

A few hours later, on the long subway ride from Brooklyn to Harlem, I'm thinking about the research and wondering if the library can really be as good as Nze says it is. When I look at her in the seat next to me, she's gazing into her phone. I know right away. Sad Nze's made her way back.

"Did I ever tell you about darker days?" she asks. "Days I wake up and everything's darker than it was the day before. Every time it happens, I realize it's happened before, but I sort of forgot, because my traitor body got used to it. So you don't even really know how far you've gone.

"Here." She hands me her phone, open to her Notes app.

> Darker Days haiku
> After the freakout
> Do the math. Six shifts this year.
> How many are left?

"That sucks so hard," I say.

"Doesn't it?"

"Any updates?" I ask.

She's always got some treatment her parents want, or some new way to try to get her dog.

"Nada," she says, and goes back to her phone.

I check mine, too, knowing now that messages come through at certain stations, where there's Wi-Fi.

Angus: Mrs. Taylor Rose offered an upgrade. Want to go to the new strato-high-end plant-based restaurant, the model for the country? She can probably get you orchestra front on Broadway, too. You in?

Chaz: Called my mom. She kind of remembers R. Taylor Rose, she's asking around to pin it down.

Me: Thanks, but don't worry about it.

At the next station:

Unknown: It is useless to tell a river to stop running; the best you can do is learn to swim in the direction it flows. By sending you Angus, I am swimming in your river. By accepting my offer, you will swim a bit in mine.

Really? Had that Angus guy just told her that I was blowing them off? Why would she even care so much? Still, I update the contact to read: "R. Taylor Rose/7 Founts."

Before the train pulls out, a new text comes in from Joelle to Nze and me.

Joelle: We won a grand! One down, five to go! WINNING FEELS SO GOOD!!!!!

Nze and I see it at the same time.

"You believe it?" I ask. "They actually won."

"Nowhere close to enough, though," Nze says. She holds up crossed fingers. "But who knows. Maybe they'll pull it off."

I can tell she wants it for them as much as I do . . . even sad Nze. We're in it with each other, Nze, Joelle, and me. Just that fast, like a little miracle.

After a minute, I text Angus.

Me: I'm in for Broadway tix, as long as I can bring my friends.

"You and I could use some wins, too," I say to Nze. If Angus can get us tix, that'd be a big one for her. And maybe the library will have a win for me.

"Here's to not darker days," Nze says.

When we finally get to the library, I'm blown away. The Schomburg Center for Research in Black Culture is more like a museum than a library. Signs for exhibits point down white-painted hallways and through glass doors. I take a picture for Mom, who'll think she died and went to Black history heaven.

A guy not much older than us, sporting shoulder-blade-length locs, takes us to the research room, which is downstairs and more like an ordinary library. The librarians are an old Black man and a younger Black woman. Just as we're telling them what we need, Joelle comes panting in, smug-grinning, like she's got pocketsful of money.

The librarian sets us up on computers to do our research and promises to do their own search on our topics. For the next two hours, the three of us barely talk to each other except to report what we're finding.

"J. M. Smith *was* pretty incredible," I say. Even though I'm annoyed that every time I search for info on the Smith school, I end up with more info on the guy himself. This says that back in the 1800s when he went to Mulberry School, the parents got together and kicked out the white principal when he wasn't treating the kids right. That's incredible for way back then. And it makes our point that Black parents have always fought and won against crazy odds for their kids' education."

Joelle turns toward me. "What? Oh . . . okay. I'm finding stuff, too. Some of these high-end schools back in the day were brutal."

"And, get this," I keep going, because I remember better when I say things out loud, even though no one's really listening. "He helped get legislation passed to integrate schools, but he made sure they kept all-Black schools open, too. So Black people would have a place of their own—which is what they were trying to do at the school my dad went to. I bet that's why they named it after him!"

"Mm-hmm. Look at this." Nze points to her own screen. "It's on that Black woman Martha Foxx. She did the first curriculum for Black blind kids, back in 1929. Can you imagine being *Black* and *blind* in *Mississippi* in *1929*?"

I try, and it's not a pretty scene. "No," I admit. "But, that woman . . . can you imagine becoming a Black blind *teacher* in Mississippi in 1929? That's pretty dope."

"I know," Nze says. I can tell she's lost in Martha Foxx's blindness, trying to figure out how she did what she did.

One of the librarians announces that there's an hour till closing, and I switch back to looking for more recent info. With everything I'm learning about schools created just so Black kids could learn their history and get support, the more I wonder about my dad. How come, if he went to this cool school that was all about learning Black history and getting empowered—how come after all that he turned out to be a deadbeat? It's more embarrassing, somehow, than just having a deadbeat dad in the first place. I move faster through screen after screen of books and articles. But I don't find what I need—nothing on the James McCune Smith High School.

A librarian's just announced the final five minutes, when the old guy from the research desk comes hobbling over, his finger in the air.

"Think I got something for you!" he says. "I cross-referenced the school with some of our collections of papers and artifacts. We have the papers of Everett Atchison, who went to J. M. Smith High School during the time you're looking for, in our archives."

"Who?" I ask. "And what's it mean, you have his papers?"

"When people do something prominent, we collect their papers, everything they might have in their estate, land deeds and manuscripts and records from schools or other institutions. This collection says that it includes high school records for Atchison, so you might find anything there—his term papers, his grades, registration records for his class—"

"Like the names of everyone who went there when he was there?" Nze asks.

"Exactly! And that was a four-year period."

"And maybe some of those people will still be in the city," Joelle says. "And we can interview them. I know I'm going to be great at the interview part."

"Will next Thursday at three p.m. work?" the librarian asks. "It's our next appointment and gives you three hours before we close."

"Thursday?" I say. "Can't we see now, even for a few minutes?"

"I'm afraid you'll be in a different building. See, the index is all we have access to here." He turns the tablet he's holding so I can see. A word catches my eye and I grab it out of his hands, more rough than I mean to.

"It says there's photos. Class photos that include 2002!"

"Yes, that makes sense. Here you are, then." He holds out an appointment card and reaches for his laptop with his other hand.

"Did you see that?" I say to Nze and Joelle. "That could mean a picture of my dad!"

"This really could be your win," Nze says, as we head to the wide stone steps outside the building. "Anyway, I gotta take the four train. I promised my mom I'd go home and try these exercises she found. Doing exercises with my *feet's* supposed to help me not fall." She shrugs and walks away.

"Meeting Chaz," Joelle says, surprising no one. She air-kisses me and takes off, too.

They have no idea, I think. After all this, they have no clue how huge it is that I might have just found a picture of my dad.

I sit on the thick marble banister of the outside stairs. 135th Street moves in front of me, cars jammed in for rush hour. Maybe I'll be able to draw how I feel tonight in my sketchbook. But I can't even wait.

I pull out a notebook.

> *Nose like mine? Lips? Feet?*
> *Or is it wishful thinking?*
> *I just need to know.*

Nze isn't the only one who can write a haiku.

NINETEEN

ZACH ON THE BEACH

"Brought you this," Zach says, maneuvering his old Toyota out of the train station parking lot and onto the street somewhere in Westport, Connecticut. He reaches behind him and hands me a purple thermos.

"Bitter mocha," he says. "I thought you might've missed it."

I open it and just the smell makes me happy. The thought of my dad's picture waiting for me at the Schomburg still burns in my belly, sending up sparks of excitement every few minutes. And even with all that, I'm glad to be here, next to Zach, headed to the water. I say thanks and take a sip.

"It's not far to the beach," Zach says. "Maybe ten minutes."

The mocha's delicious, and I'm in mid suck-down, so I don't say anything. Zach's hair's a little longer, and he's tanned from his beach job. And he seems relaxed, in a way I'm not used to. Like maybe more relaxed than me. He reaches for the music and "Soul Food y Adobo" comes on. I don't remember if he knows I like it or if it's just a coincidence. Either way, it's nice, and I finally settle back and enjoy my drink.

"Do you want to stop anywhere before we get there?" Zach asks, after a while.

"I'm good," I say. "The coffee's really nice."

"I'm glad," he says. "And look, we're here."

He pulls into a parking lot, the usual kind with a little kiosk where you pay, and the guy directs us to a spot. I can already see the sand and the wide expanse of sky that says you're almost there. The smell of the ocean takes over the second I open my door.

"How do you know about this place?" I ask.

"My sister goes to Quinnipiac University," he says. "Long story, since you'd think UMass would be cheaper, but she wanted this specific program. Anyway, my mom made us come out here all the time her first year, and I drove around a lot while they hung out."

"You didn't want to visit your sister?" I ask, while Zach grabs a milk crate filled with beach stuff from his trunk. He slams it shut, and we head to the path through the dunes.

"I visited her a couple times without my parents," he says. "I only went on their trips because I like to drive and they hate it. And I got to find places like this."

The beach is in sight now, and it's long and curved and just the right amount of rocky. Only a few scattered blankets so far, and I can't see anybody in the water.

"You pick the spot," Zach says, so I lead us right down to the

167

water, and Zach unloads his blanket and a couple of plastic bags, which have chips and sodas, beach toys, and a Bluetooth speaker. The boy's going all out, no question.

We sit on the blanket, leaning back on our elbows.

It's beautiful, sunny and hot. It's as good as I thought it would be, seeing Zach. Before I can think too much about what all that means, he leans over and kisses me. A nice kiss, which he breaks off before it gets deep. Like the music in the car, it chills me out, and I lay back all the way. I have on a wrap dress over my bathing suit, and I open it and let the sun dance all over me.

"Is it as good as Gloucester?" he asks.

"Sure," I say. "The regular beach. I just love the cove by my house. It's not this pretty, but nobody really goes back there, even my mom. It's always peaceful. And it's right there for me, no matter what. It feels like it's mine."

"Poetic," Zach says, not as a joke. "I felt like that once, when we visited Cape Verde."

I prop up to look at him. "When did you go?"

"The first time when I was eight. I remember thinking that the whole place—well, not that it belonged to me. But that maybe I belonged to it? I just felt connected, like I was a part of the place and nobody could tell me to get out. I loved that feeling."

"I don't think I get all that from my cove."

"Yeah . . ."

"I get a lot, though . . ."

After a while, he sticks a hand in his pocket and pulls out a rock. "I brought you something else," he says. "It's from my collection.

I've only got to go to Cape Verde twice, because it's expensive, but my mom goes back a lot because we still own property with some of her brothers. Every time she goes, she brings me a rock. I thought . . . you're probably not the kind of girl who wants a stuffed bear . . ."

I take the rock, which is smooth and layered and warm from his pocket.

"Your mom brings you rocks?"

"It's a tradition now, from when I was little."

"What else?" I ask. "About your family."

I've wondered about them ever since he told me on the phone how they were such a range of Black. I lie back down to listen, stroking the rock in one hand.

"They're just regular immigrants, I guess. My parents work; they want to get ahead. They maybe should be divorced, but what else is new? Maybe when my little sister graduates, they'll be one of those couples that starts having affairs at a hundred years old. But we're okay."

"How come you moved to Gloucester from Boston?" I ask. I can tell he likes that I'm asking questions for a change.

"For the schools," he says. "And it's good for business because of the tourists."

"My mom says the same thing," I say, thinking of her and all the parents we're learning about for our article. "She moved us to Gloucester for the schools. And, at least back then, it was cheaper. I don't get her, though. There must've been other places she could've gone. If you're all into Black history and Black pride, which she is, why move to Gloucester, where the only Black faces we see are on our own walls, or at Marley's stupid parties?"

Zach's eyes widen, and I realize what I said. "Oh! I didn't mean . . ."

"Yeah, you did," he says.

I don't bother denying it.

"People have their reasons for moving places," Zach says. "Like, Marley's family moved to Gloucester because her dad lost his job in Chicago. They wanted someplace where they had family close, and we already had cousins in Rockport."

"Yeah. It was a big deal for her dad, losing his job."

"She told you about it?" Zach looks surprised.

"If you weren't around to hang with," I say. "I spent a lot of time skulking in corners at Marley's parties. This one time, I'd gone in the pantry, and Marley's dad and uncles came and sat around the kitchen table."

I remember, I must've been about ten years old. Marley's dad had been scared he was going to lose his job again. I'd peeked out and seen his head bent as he talked, like he was telling it all to the saltshaker. The rest of the grown-ups leaned toward him, listening. When he was done, they said he was too good to get fired, but if he did, they had money he could borrow. While they talked, they scooched their chairs closer to him and each other. Her dad's head lifted. They all ended up laughing.

It made me want things I'd never had, seeing all those people having his back, just because they're family. And it made me scared, like being on the outside when you can see how warm and good the inside is.

Since I don't want to say all this to Zach, I flip over and lie down with my head on my arms. I get the not-awful feeling that he's just looking at me.

"What?" I say, after a minute.

"I thought now might be the time you wanna tell me what's up with you and Marley."

I consider it—the reasons I understand and the ones I don't. "Did you know she was queer?" I ask.

"Yeah. You didn't?"

I squirm. "It's so like her not to bother coming out. To just start showing up places with her girlfriend."

"You don't think it's kind of brave?" Zach asks.

I roll my eyes. "I just don't think of Marley as brave. That's the main thing I don't like about her, she doesn't really *try* much. She just lets things happen. It's annoying, and it's even worse when Black people do it because we can't afford not to try. My mom says, if you don't have a seat at the table, you're probably on the menu. So you *have* to go for the table."

When Zach doesn't say anything, I lift my head to get a better look at him.

"That's what you think of me, too? I'm on the menu?"

"What? No!" And then I'm sitting up again, realizing that I do think that, a little bit, and I definitely didn't mean to let him know it. "I thought we were talking about Marley," I say.

"Well, I'm not," he says, ignoring me. "On the menu. I just don't like to be in people's faces all the time. You don't have to be *loud* or . . . or *obvious*, to try. I think it's the same for Marley. And if you think I don't have any choices in terms of girls, trust me, I've got plenty of choices."

He looks indignant and adorable with the sun shining on his kinky curls. To shut him up, I kiss him, a long warm kiss. Zach catches on quick to the change of subject and runs his fingers down my sweaty back. I break it off, not because it isn't fun. Maybe because it's too fun and I already have a lot to think about.

We settle into new positions, weight on our elbows, facing each other. Easier, now. Zach sprinkles sand on my shoulder. I wonder how I can like him as much as I do and still like Bolt. But I'm thinking about Marley, too, and how her dad's been such a big part of why I've been jealous of her so long.

I don't know what I'll do about Zach and Bolt. Whatever it is will have to wait till I figure out about the FGS and my dad.

TWENTY

SIX!

"This is . . . perfect," Nze whispers. "We're right by the stage steps. Do you see how perfect this is?"

I really do. Nze, Joelle, Angus, and I are sitting in the front row of an actual Broadway theater, compliments of R. Taylor Rose. After the beach, I can't help wishing it was Zach here with us instead of Angus, but I resist texting him.

My eyes dart from the high ceilings and chandeliers to the gilded woodwork to the gold-banistered balcony overhead. The lights are low and the crowd on fire, so it feels like we're in some kind of portal waiting for the door to open on the other side. And, still, the best part is Nze.

She's turned back around, her eyes glued to the purple velvet curtain at the front of the stage. We've been over the plan fifty times. The second the show ends, she says she's desperate to pee and pushes her way out to the aisle before anybody else moves. I pretend I lost my phone, to distract Angus. And while nobody's looking, Nze makes a run for the stage. She gets to the center, throws out her arms and shouts, "Thank you! Thank you very much!" which Joelle, who's sitting on her other side, gets on video. That's it. By the time the staff try to get her down from there, it'll be done.

"The only thing that could go wrong is *him*," she whispers, still eyeing the stage but head-pointing to Angus, who's sitting on my other side. "Can't you get him to leave early?"

"He's not gonna know it's happening till it's done," I tell her, glancing at Angus, who's leaning over in his seat, getting buddy-buddy with the people next to him.

Nze doesn't look convinced, but she leaves it alone. Behind us, the theater's filling up.

"Now, I heard Anna was the best queen," Angus says to the white woman on *his* left. "Doesn't she do that dirty rascal song?"

"Well, my favorite's Jane," says the woman. "But I brought my daughter and her friends last time, and they adored Anna."

She goes back to reading her program, and Angus turns to me. "Aren't you glad you said yes?"

I shrug, because he doesn't need to know the rush I've felt since I saw the marquee outside and watched the staff guy lift the velvet rope for us.

It touches my own excitement about seeing the picture of my dad. I flash back to sitting in the Checkerboard Bistro, feeling the same excitement. And a pit opens in me. It could happen all over again, I could get screwed, disappointed. My heart broken.

174

In the theater, a sound like a giant switch being thrown echoes over us. The lights go out, and a hush settles before a deep voice welcomes us in the darkness. A second later, the music starts, and the curtain slowly rises. Nze squeezes my hand. Joelle squeals. Angus lets out an eager grunt. I give in to the mood.

Six women in silhouette stand on the stage. Then the lights go up, and there's so much glitz I can't help blinking. They're wearing the brightest, most dazzling costumes I can imagine. And they can dance. They're the six wives of Henry the Eighth, except they're all different races and they're wearing badass boots and short dresses or tight pants, all of it jewel-studded and glittering under the lights. They start to sing.

Welcome to the show, to the his-to-re-mix . . .

The music matches the glitz, and the energy's off the chain, and I get lost in watching, listening, feeling so close I'm in it.

"That's the really famous one," Nze whispers a while later, pointing at the woman in the cutest costume, who's taking center stage. "Anne Boleyn. The first one who got beheaded."

"I know!" I whisper, waving a hand to shush her.

Angus shouts whenever there's a serious dance move, Nze keeps commenting on the lyrics, and Joelle can't shut up about the costumes. I try to ignore them. I'm a pissed-off ex-wife of Henry the Eighth, one of the six queens, singing about what a dick Henry is—except instead of a fifteenth-century white woman in skirts and corsets, I'm one of the two Black women up there, killing it in tight sequined leggings and kick-ass boots. It's beautiful, how they each tell a whole story in one song, how it makes you think about this piece of history you kind of knew but not really. *Their* piece of history—the bitchy one, the one who was abused since she was a kid, the one who loved him back. The best is the one Henry thought he blew off but who got to divorce him and be the queen of her very own castle.

I'm still in the fifteenth century when Nze grabs my arm and whispers, "This is the last number. *It's almost time.*"

"What?" I ask.

She squeezes harder.

"It's almost over!" she hisses. "I have to go up soon!"

Onstage, the queens start literally singing about how they only have five more minutes.

Too many years, lost in his story

Shit. I look around at the fancy rapt crowd. Are we all gonna get arrested for, like, trespassing on a Broadway stage? Or just Nze could get arrested and she'd be all by herself, and we wouldn't even know how to call her parents. I lean over to Joelle to see if she's ready to shove back so Nze can pass her, then run interference if anything happens while I'm keeping Angus busy looking for my phone. She nods, but looks scared, too.

"For four more minutes . . . ," sing the queens.

"Maybe I should go out to the aisle now, before everybody stands up," Nze whispers.

But Joelle shakes her head.

"That'll just draw attention," she snaps. We stare at each other, leaning forward in our seats. Suddenly, there's applause like thunder. Up on the stage, the queens are taking bows. The curtain goes down.

Holy shit. "Go!" I whisper.

But Nze shakes her head.

"Curtain call," she moans. "I forgot!"

I have no idea what she's talking about. But the curtain goes up again, and there are the queens. They start a whole other song.

Nze yells in my ear, "Just stay ready." She's got her body in starter position, bent forward in her seat, one foot in front of the other, like an Olympic skater. Finally, the audience is clapping again and the curtain's falling. Instantly, people stand up.

"Bathroom!" Nze shouts, slipping past Joelle to the aisle on the right. And it's happening.

I gulp, drop my phone behind my seat, just as Angus says, "Come on, now that was good!"

"I can't find my phone!" I say, squatting down to pretend to look for it.

From down on the floor, I can hear Joelle muttering, "It's gonna be fine. . . ."

"Got it!" Angus shouts, tapping me on the shoulder with the phone, making me wish I'd dropped it farther away. I stand and don't even look at him. Nze isn't on the stage. I look to the right and don't see her anywhere.

"Take it!" Angus says, waving my phone at me. "Let's go."

"Just wait!" I say, taking the phone.

"For what?" Angus says. "We can meet your friend outside."

He starts moving left, just as I catch sight of Nze running up the stairs. A second later, she's runway-walking toward center stage. She's wearing boots, even though it's July, and a tight-fitting shirt over jeans. She stands with her legs apart and her hands on her hips. Joelle and I stare at her, and Angus seems to get that something's happening.

"What the hell?" he starts. I feel him follow our gaze, up to the stage. To be sure he doesn't try to go after her, I loop my arm through his.

"Please, just shut up!" I say, staring up at Nze. *Why's she just standing there, not saying her thing?* She's gonna get stopped any second.

Angus starts to complain. There's a shout from the right side of the theater. An usher is moving toward the stage stairs. "Off the stage, now, girl! Audience members aren't allowed up there!"

Nze's head swivels in his direction, then faces front again. She throws out her arms and starts to . . . *sing.* Complete with sound effects.

I'm the queen of the castle . . .

"Get down!" the usher yells, running up the stage stairs. "Get the hell down from there!"

With one last, *boom boom!* Nze folds an arm across her middle and takes a bow. Then she turns and fast-walks—but doesn't run—off the other side of the stage. The usher is on her heels.

"What should we do?" Joelle yells. "Oh my God, what should we do?"

"What is going on?!" Angus demands.

Nze has her hands up like the usher's a cop, and I can tell she's saying she's done, she'll leave, nothing to worry about. The usher's chin points toward a side door, and he shouts for people to move aside so he can lead Nze through.

"I guess we should follow her?" I say.

"Or meet her at the police station," Angus mumbles.

But when we get to the hallway, there's no way to know where she's gone, and the crowd is too thick to maneuver much. We agree to wait outside to see if she calls us.

"That was so incredibly stupid," Angus says, when we're on the sidewalk.

"Let's let the crowd die down," Joelle says anxiously. "And if she doesn't come out, we can go back in and find her."

People start to huddle up outside the theater, talking about the show. And then a voice shouts from behind us. "That was the shiiiit!"

Nze's there, beaming brighter than the costumes. "Could you tell how many people were looking at me? Even before I started singing! And once I started, I had the whole room!"

"So, they're just letting you go?" Angus asks.

"I talked him down," Nze says, shrugging like it was nothing. She's the happiest I've ever seen her.

I wonder if this R. Taylor Rose person may know what she's doing after all.

TWENTY-ONE

DEEP LIKE THE RIVERS

"Remember, we have to be fast," I say. "We can't be late for our appointment!"

Nze, Joelle, and I are standing in the fancy foyer of the Schomburg Center, Nze singing about being queen of the castle, and Joelle wedding texting, while I sweat.

In twenty minutes, I'll see my dad's photo. But because we're early and Nze's a bigger nerd than I thought, we're waiting to see Langston Hughes's ashes.

My phone dings, and I'm glad for the distraction. But it's Zach, who I've been blowing off since our beach day because Bolt's been texting a lot and I don't know how to like two boys at once.

Zach: Since you're so busy, I'll have to be corny in writing. Will you go to Marley's party with me?

He sends a pic of an old-fashioned corsage.

Zach, Zach, Zach, I think.

"Please. Just do it!" Nze says, looking over my shoulder. "You said he's a good kisser."

"He is," I say. "And a good guy. But liking him's a lot right now. He's too far away to even see. And there's Bolt, so . . ."

"So, nothing," Nze says. "Just be glad you like people who like you back." When she puts it that way, it does seem nice to just go with it.

"Maybe you're right," I say.

Me: Sure! Thanks.

"Okay, ladies, right this way!" One of the black-suited guides leads us down a hallway to golden doors that open on an area so big, it's more of a courtyard than a room.

"Who knew you could have your ashes buried in a library," Joelle says. Other than Nze, I think, probably only my mother.

The room has a shiny white floor with a beautiful circular design in shades of red and brown in the middle.

"He's buried under that?" Nze asks, pointing to the artwork.

"His ashes are," the guy says. "And this art here, this is called a cosmogram. It's to honor both Langston Hughes and Arthur Schomburg, who, of course, started this center."

I move closer. At the very center of the giant circle design are the words: *My soul has grown deep like the rivers.*

"That's just a coincidence, right?" I ask, pointing to the last word.

Joelle squats, reaches a hand out over the swirl of reds and browns. "Nothing here's a coincidence," she says. "This thing is full of messages and emotions."

I take a picture for my mom with the caption: *Langston Hughes's ashes are actually under here.* As I type Langston's name, I suddenly remember that Marley did a paper on him a couple of years ago—an assignment our moms made us work on together. In a rush of good energy, I send a pic to Marley, too, adding, *Remembered you liked his poetry.*

It feels decent, reaching out to her. But then I notice the time.

"Let's go, come on!" I head for the door before Nze or Joelle can even answer.

They follow. Finally, we're going to the section where we have our appointment.

"We're looking for information on James McCune Smith High School," I tell the librarian, who doesn't look that much older than us. "And, specifically, this guy Everett Atchison who went to the school." I tell them about the photo we saw listed and ask to see it. Joelle requests more info on the Palmer Academy, the first Black boarding school for rich kids. Nze asks about Martha Foxx, the Black woman who started the academy for the blind.

"But hers first," Nze says, pointing to me.

"Gotcha," says the librarian. He sets me up with a digital collection on one of their desktops. There's a long list of materials you can click on. The page is actually called "The Negroes of New York Collection."

"You should find that photograph here," the librarian says, pointing to a link called prints and photographs.

With a glance at Nze and Joelle, I click. A new list comes up, and the librarian points again.

"And then here," he says.

I click.

There it is. I enlarge as much as I can and devour the screen with my eyes, homing in on all the kids. "Do any of them look like me?" I ask.

"Shrink the screen," Joelle says. "Maybe there's a caption?"

And there is. Third from the left in the second row is Richard Bryant. Now that I know where to find him, I'm slow to look. Shy. Like we'll be meeting.

"He's kinda hot," Nze says. "Nice fade, pretty eyes."

"So does he?" I ask again. "Look like me?"

"Turn around, let us see you together," Nze says. Their eyes travel between the screen and my face. Nze breaks into a grin.

"I see it!" she says. "In the brows and in your noses, too. I really see it!"

Finally, I look at Richard Bryant's face. He has strong features, nice eyes, like Nze said. Do they turn up at the corners, like mine? It's hard to tell. The photo's small, and it's weird that he's my age, not dad-aged. I study his brows and nose, his cheeks and ears, and I think I see something familiar. A little bit.

"Let's get you a copy," Joelle says, going off to get the librarian. I stay still awhile, smiling at the picture. Whether he looks like me or not, this is huge. Because the thing is . . . he has *a face*. He's real.

"When you're ready," Nze says, "I saw the word *McCune* on that first list. There could be more good stuff."

I nod, swallow. Take a picture of the photo and navigate back to the list.

"Wait a sec." Nze leans over my shoulder, laying a finger on the screen. "See this neighborhood where McCune's school was, *Five Points*? And remember I told you about *Paradise Square*, the best Black play on Broadway? Well, that play is set in *that neighborhood*—Five Points!

"Maybe there's a way to fit it in our project?" she says. "We could even do a podcast so we can include some of the music, for background. . . ."

"Sure," I say. "Can we keep going?"

On the list, there are entries for this guy Everett Atchison's life: "Early Life and Family," "Contributions in Mathematics," "Early Education," and finally . . . "*McCune High School.*"

I click it. There are blank forms, student papers, attendance records. We scroll through those looking for the name Richard Bryant but don't find him. We click on a file called "Courses and Syllabi." There's something called the "Freedom Summer Curriculum" collection. We click again. A student paper catches my eye. Except it's not what I thought it would be: "'Lessons We Can Learn from the Struggles of the 1960s,' *by Everett Atchison and Asha Mitchell.*"

"Keep scrolling," Joelle says. "I bet there's stuff we can use in there."

She doesn't get it, of course. She knows we're looking for Richard Bryant, my dad's name. She doesn't get how weird it is that we just found my mom's name.

Because my mom went to some "ordinary public school." That's what she said when I've asked how high school was for her. "Good enough, but nothing special."

I point at the page. "That's my mom's name," I say in a flat voice. *"My mom went to this school."*

"Your mom?" Joelle says. "Oh, it's probably where they met. That makes sense."

She makes it sound so logical. I guess it would be if my mom hadn't lied. And now it's so much more. It's a window into her past that she tried to lock shut. I could open it. I could find out stuff about her that she never wanted me to know.

I stand to shake off some energy. What does it *mean*, that my mom's name is here?

The ring is the clue Uncle Wendell gave me, and this school is what it leads to. Mom went to this school, which makes the trail lead back to her, in a way. Mom . . . who won't talk.

It's like my mystery history is right here in front of me and every time I reach for it, it twists out of my grasp.

TWENTY-TWO

LIES ARE BULLSHIT

"I barely recall supper last night, young woman! Do I look like I'd remember somebody I met nearly twenty years ago?" It's the old Black guy I saw last time I was at River Room. I'm holding my phone out to him, open to the photo of my dad's class picture, zoomed in on his face.

It's late, just a couple hours till curfew, but after everything that happened at the library yesterday, I had to come.

"Could you just try?" I ask. The guy's tall and straight-backed, and he's already told me he worked here "since we opened, back in '96." There's a jingling sound as he empties tokens out of a machine. He puts the money in the big pocket at the front of his apron, then lifts his glasses up his nose and bends over my phone.

"I won't say he doesn't look familiar," he says. "Good-looking boy. We didn't get too many Black kids back in those days. But I can't say I remember him, either."

"Sure, I get it," I say. I pull up a different photo and cross my fingers against the back of the phone.

"What about her?" I ask. "She'd've been a teenager, too. I just don't have a picture from back then."

"That's you?" he asks. I nod. My best picture of my mom shows the two of us together at a tearoom in Boston, after we'd got our hair done. "Same 'maybe' as I gave you before," he says. "Sorry."

I know he's done with me, but I'm not ready to give up. I try one of mom's looks—my face perfectly calm, but a little hard—the one she uses for waitstaff who need to up their service game. The guy only shrugs, says, "I'd help if I could." And moves to the next machine.

I thank him and head to the counter. There was hardly any chance he was going to say what I wanted: *Yeah, sure, Asha! Of course I remember* . . . But if he had, I could've started a conversation with Mom in a way that wasn't torture. *Crazy coincidence! I met this guy who knew you. . . .*

It's weak—but it's *something*.

The place smells more like beer than cheese at this hour, but I grab a stool anyway. It's only a week till I go home for Marley's party, and I know I have to talk to Mom. Because if the FGS is bull and the ring leads me back to her, what choice do I have? The closer it gets, though, the more I dread the conversation.

"Brave of you, giving me a chance to steal your title," a voice says.

I turn, and Bolt's next to me. I'd forgotten I'd texted him to meet me here. He bends and kisses me on the cheek, catching some lip. It's nice. And he doesn't step back after the kiss. "Not worried," I say. We smile at each other a minute before he takes the stool next to mine.

Maybe it's all the mess with Mom, but after the last time he texted, all I wanted was to be real with him. And I know, just from how it feels to have him close that I made the right call, inviting him here. I'd had fun when we were here before, and I'd gotten mad, too. I'd had feelings that were just about him—separate from stressing over blue building and the FGS. So, if we're going to figure out whatever it is between us, this is the place to do it.

I look back at the old guy, who's still collecting tokens from the machines. There's nothing else I can do here to get the information I want. I focus on Bolt, who, for some reason, reminds me of coffee-shop Bolt tonight. He looks . . . vulnerable. His head a little ducked, his smile shy. Like maybe it wasn't that easy for him to come here after I've been blowing him off for a while.

"I really like you," I blurt out. I didn't know I was going to say it, but it's good.

He hesitates, then leans in. Stops an inch in front of my mouth in case I want to say no. Instead, I close the gap. He makes a little sound, like eating good cake, and puts his hands on my waist. It's not a long kiss since we're at the counter. But enough to know I have another good kisser on my hands.

When we pull away, his lopsided grin is back. "Skee-Ball?" he says.

I shake my head.

"Can we just talk?" I ask. I look into his face and all I know is, the truth matters. Lies are bullshit. And I haven't been telling him the truth.

"My grandma doesn't live over near you," I say. "I thought she might. I was hoping. But . . . it wasn't true when I said she lived there." I wanted to say "I lied," but it doesn't come out that way.

Bolt looks confused.

"Why would you lie about where your grandma lives?" he asks.

"Because I'd . . . *already been* lying about it," I say. "It was why I was hanging out over there, to try and figure out who was in apartment twenty-two. I knew the person there had been sending stuff to my house. Long story . . ."

"This have to do with what you told me about your dad?"

"Yeah."

"So, you were trying to figure out who lived there?" he says. "Are you saying . . . you were using me to find stuff out?"

"I know I like you," I say again. Because that's true at least. "I did the whole time."

Bolt slow-nods.

"And there's also a guy at home . . . ," I say.

He raises his eyebrows.

"It's not a total thing," I say. "We never said we were exclusive . . . I just wanted to tell you."

"Huh," he says. "Anything else?"

"Nope, zero."

He gives me another kiss. It's longer and nicer. After a while, he pulls away the tiniest bit, inviting me to come in for more. If it's a test, I guess I pass.

"Skee-Ball?" he asks again, when it's over.

I grin and lead the way.

TWENTY-THREE

JUJU GOO

"I have a surprise!" Joelle says. "Before the two of you take off on your big adventure."

The three of us are in her dorm room, which seems extra sunny with the curtains open.

"I can't believe I *am* going," Nze says. "I thought the beach vigil was gonna be the hardest thing on my list. I couldn't figure out how to stay on the beach all night without getting attacked."

"Marley Evans to the rescue," I mutter.

I hadn't put it together that Marley's party would give Nze a chance to do the "beach vigil" on her list. But when I started complaining to her about the party, she put it together quick. Now I have to deal with Nze seeing my boring Gloucester life, meeting Roxy. And Marley. But it's happening, so . . .

"Let's get to it," Joelle says, getting us to settle down on the pillows. Instead of snacks, her low table has a big glass jar of something gold-colored sitting in the middle. "We're all stressed, right? Everything's going down soon, and we have to deal. I still have four thousand, two hundred dollars to make before I can get my dress, plus the cupcake guy wants to give us sloppy seconds. Nze's parents are doubling down on this new treatment they found in Mexico. And Clae, you have to go face your mom with all this stuff you found."

"Not to mention Zach and Marley," I say.

"So we all need to tune into what's going on inside us," Joelle says. "In order to make good decisions." She drops a hand on the glass jar. "That's where this comes in.

"The problem with empathic people, which is all of us to some degree, is we're so busy feeling everybody else's feelings that we don't always feel our own. So"—she waves ta-da hands over the jar—"juju goo! Homemade salt-and-honey scrub. It cleanses away other people's annoying juju so we can feel our own."

"What do we do with it?" I ask.

"Best is to shower with it," she says, "but you don't have to do full body. Today, we're just gonna go in the bathroom and do our chests and bellies, that's the most important. Then, we'll do our activity."

Nze's got this confused but amused look on her face that has to irritate Joelle.

"How do you know about this?" Nze asks.

"It's called study," Joelle says. "My teacher is excellent. And nobody's making you do it."

"No, I want to!" Nze says quickly. "Sorry. Is the bathroom part now?" She stands up.

"Yeah, we do the goo first, then come back and talk."

We head down the hall to one of the dorm bathrooms, which has six sinks, toilets, and shower stalls. Above the sinks there's a long mirror and a ledge to put your stuff on. Joelle opens the jar and sets it on the ledge. The earthy sweet smell of honey fills the room.

Looking at us in the mirror, Joelle peels off her shirt, turns on the tap, and starts smearing the stuff in the jar all over herself. "Like this," she says, demonstrating. "Your heart, chest, neck, and belly are most important. But then armpits are good, too, and since I'm doing those, I like to do my whole arms. It's good for your skin, anyhow."

Nze and I pull off our shirts, and I try not to be distracted by the fact that this is our first time undressing in front of each other.

"Hoo, it's kind of scratchy!" Nze says, sticking a handful of scrub between her boobs. A second later, she's unhooked her bra, and she's *all* boobs. Full and heavy, so different from mine. I take off my bra too and spread the goo all over. It reminds me of when Roxy and I used to play in the mud. It feels fun and a little wrong.

"Good," Joelle says, neatly gooing around and under her still-on bra. "Don't forget the back of your neck and shoulders. We can help each other get it off." She goes to a rack of cubbies and hands us each a small towel. "When you feel ready, just wet the towel and clean it off."

We finish smearing, then start washing it off. Afterward, I feel good but exposed. And lighter, like I washed off a layer of soot I didn't know was there. We put our shirts on and go back to Joelle's room.

"This is simple," Joelle says. "It's just first thought, best thought, only better because it's after we've cleansed. We sit in a circle and take index cards and pens." She gets the supplies out of her desk. "And we take turns asking each other questions and then writing down our first thought. Okay, so first we take a minute to think of the best questions for each other. You can write those down, too, if you want, so you don't forget."

I think about my friends. I know just what to ask Joelle, but Nze's super hard.

"We don't have to say the answer out loud?" Nze asks. "Just write it down?"

"Exactly."

"Then, I'm ready," Nze says. "Ask me something."

Joelle nods. "Here it is. If you get the treatment and it goes bad, how will you be okay?"

"*What?*" Nze looks terrified.

Joelle repeats it.

Nze bends her head, and for a long time, nothing happens. Finally, she writes on her card.

"Perfect!" Joelle beams as Nze raises her head, looking relieved. "Clae, you want to do a question for me, and then we'll just keep going around till we run out of questions?"

This one I'm ready for. "Joelle, what's the plan if you can't afford the dress?"

Joelle looks kind of sick but not surprised. She writes something on her card. "Now, Nze, you ask Clae a question."

"Got it," Nze says. "Clae, when are you gonna talk to your mom, and what are you gonna say?"

I know it's the right question. I even know, deep down, that I have an answer. I squeeze my eyes closed a minute, picturing me, home with Mom. What do I want to say to her? How do I want it to be?

Something opens in me, and I start writing—not thinking, just writing:

I'm going to tell her I love her. And thank her for raising me alone. I'm going to show her the ring, and tell her that Uncle Wendell wanted me to know about my dad. And I'm going to ask her to please tell me her story.

I'm going to do it on Sunday, after the party.

"Done," I say, and hear the shake in my voice. "Who's next?"

TWENTY-FOUR

POD'S AND JERRY'S

I can't stop staring at Nze as the Greyhound pulls off the highway and into Gloucester. She's got on cotton overalls and her Docs, hair in fresh box braids, all very *not* Gloucester. She actually looks fascinated by what she's seeing out the window, which is literally nothing if you don't count trees. I'm nervous on so many levels—it's easiest to focus on how it'll feel to show her my regular life.

"You ready for this?" I ask.

"Please," she says. "I get a major check off my list, *and* I get your mom's legendary cooking?" The bus turns into the station.

"Gloucester!" the driver announces. "Gather your belongings and check your seat. . . ."

"And there's Mom," I mutter. She's in the parking lot, standing beside our car. She squints at the bus windows, then heads toward us. Nze waves out the window.

"Hurry up, go!" she says, already on her feet.

Then we're down the aisle and through the doors. The smell of Gloucester—fresh wind and fried fish and salt—is in my nose, so familiar it aches. Mom's there, hugging me like she hasn't seen me in a year.

"This is Nze," I say, pulling away. Nze goes straight for the hug, smile on extreme beam.

When Mom pulls back, she looks happier than I can remember seeing her.

"Girls!" she says. "I know you want to hang out with Roxy and all your friends, but you have to eat, so I made dinner at the house first. Is that okay?"

Mom starts talking about everything we can see from the parking lot, which is still nothing. In the car, Nze leans forward from the back seat, asking questions, and Mom throws me a smug look. *You have a Black friend!* I lean back on the seat, close my eyes, and try to let the feels settle.

"Oh, and we're about to pass the yacht club," Mom says, heading up Main Street. "Where you all will be going tonight." We get closer, and I see that the club's already decked out with party lights. There's a banner out front that reads, *Welcome to Pod's and Jerry's.*

"Is that for your friend's thing?" Nze asks. "You didn't say it was a twenties theme."

"You recognized the name!" Mom says, sending me an even smugger look.

"It's famous in New York," Nze says. "I mean if you study Black history. Billie Holiday sang there."

196

I don't have a clue what they're talking about, and I tell them so.

Mom looks over at me, her brow scrunched up. "What do you mean?" she asks.

I stare at her as she turns onto our street and pulls into the driveway. She shuts off the ignition and faces me.

"It's been all Marley's mom's talked about for weeks. It's on the invitation, they're doing costumes, music, games— everything from the nineteen twenties."

Nze pops her head between our seats. "Costumes?" she says. "We were supposed to do costumes?"

"That's ridiculous!" I say, realizing I never actually opened the invitation. "Look, we don't have to go, just because we came home . . ."

"We'll figure it out," Mom says. "I'll see what I can do while you have some food." I don't take the new development as a *good* omen.

"In New York," Nze says, looking at our house as we get out of the car, "this would be a palace. You know that, right?"

Mom beams as she leads us to the door. I stop halfway up the walkway, overwhelmed by way too many feelings. It's like everything I've ever worried about in this house—Mom keeping secrets, me keeping things from Roxy, tests, and contests, and grades—all that anxiousness I carry around when I'm here is waiting for me to put it on like a too-heavy coat. But the coat—it's warm and cozy, too. For all the times I've shut that door behind me and felt safe.

"Come on!" Mom calls. "Get in here. I have a great idea!"

I walk in and smell garlic tomato sauce and melting chocolate. My stomach growls as the coat settles on my shoulders.

Two hours later, we're fed, Roxy's on her way over, and Nze and I are finishing with our outfits.

"I didn't see this coming," I tell Mom, looking in the full-length mirror she's pulled into the living room along with all our costume junk. I've got on two of her silky summer nightgowns—one longer, one shorter, so they look layered, both cream-colored and pinned so they hug my curves. It actually looks nice.

"Go on and pretend it doesn't work," Mom says, brows up and smiling because she knows she did good. She's in such an up place, it's weirding me out.

"It's the pearls that do it," she says. "And the flapper headbands, of course. Now you see why I keep a fabric box."

Nze nudges me away from the mirror so she can check herself out in Mom's gold silk robe, open and beltless over my too-tight-on-her camisole and her own jeans. It's her hair that makes it work—Mom's got it gathered into a one-sided bun just above her shoulder, a gold flapper band holding it tight against her forehead, with a royal-blue fabric feather, just like my cream one, stuck in the side. She flips her long pearls at me.

"All right," Mom says. "I need a few minutes with my Clae Baby before the festivities. Nze, sweetheart, make yourself at home."

I send Nze a *Save me* look, but Mom's already pulling me out of the room and up the stairs. We go into her room, and she closes the door, sits on the bed, and waits for me to sit, too.

"You will be out all night and then you're going to sleep through tomorrow," she says. "So, I'm getting my time in while I can."

The room smells like hospital antiseptic, which accumulates in her hamper. Stepping in, I think of Roxy, going through her files. And my dad's medical records. I think of Mom's name on a high school paper and how I said I'd talk to her on Sunday, put it all out there. But can I?

We sit on the bed, and Mom purses her lips, before talking. "I just . . . I didn't feel so great about that conversation we had when you were asking about your uncle Wendell. I thought about it. He was a kind of father figure for you, wasn't he? He'd have to be, considering. I should have made sure you spent more time with him, even if . . . he had his issues. So I wanted to tell you, I see that now. And I'm sorry. Even though he's gone, I can give you more memories of him and help you know him better, like you were asking for. Could that help?"

This is so out of nowhere I don't know what to say. "Sure, Mom."

"I just want you to know that I approve," she says. "It's good you feel that way about your uncle, because your father—there's just no point in holding that spot, that paternal place in your heart for him. He wouldn't deserve it. So, good on you for lifting up your uncle. All right? You understand?"

I understand she can't quit dissing my dad. But what she's saying about Uncle Wendell makes what I'm planning to tell her seem more possible. Leaning back on my elbows, I get a memory of how much I loved being in here when I was little. It always felt special, with its grown-up smell and all her bottles and jars and jewelry laid out on the dresser.

"Now," she says, her face lighting up. "Tell me about your new friend!" But before I can, car lights flash across the room. Roxy's pulling into the driveway.

We both get up, and Mom glances back at me.

"Oh," she says. "Before I forget, there's mail for you, I put it in your room. I think there's something from one of the programs you applied to for next year."

A minute later, we're downstairs at the door and Roxy's coming in with a goofy-looking blond dude behind her.

"This is, um, Liam," she says. She looks hot in a tight black fringe dress, her red hair loose and glossy under her flapper band.

I don't think I've ever seen her so nervous. Liam's got slicked-back twenties-style hair, round glasses, and a suit jacket and skinny tie over shiny black pants. He looks like a nerdy guy from now, trying to look like a nerdy guy from a hundred years ago.

It's dark outside and warm. We all head to Roxy's Prius with our overnight bags, Mom shooing us out so she can get dressed and come, too.

The car feels off, because Liam's in my usual seat, up front with Roxy, me and Nze in the back. But Roxy's so nervous about us meeting Liam that I don't worry too much about her meeting Nze. Liam's the first to talk.

"It's been a minute, you know?" he says. "For me, going to a high school party. You know, since I'm in college. Roxy thought I was even older than I am, you know, since I'm the manager at the store. Well, I don't know if you do know . . ." He looks back at us.

"*We know!*" Nze says. "And *you know* what? I *know* what you mean."

I'm glad she's happy Nze tonight, because it comes out funny instead of nasty. She leans up between the seats.

"You know what else, Liam? Maybe you can stick with me tonight? I'm the new kid, which is much harder than being, you know, the older guy."

"I can do that for you," Liam says.

Roxy turns on music, too loud to talk over, and Olivia Rodrigo fills the car. Nze sits back, grinning. I close my eyes. Now that we're on our way, the tingles in my stomach are popping off like lit sparklers. Finally, I can think about what happens next. Marley. And Zach. How do I tell him I kissed another guy and told him I liked him? I don't want to lie. And I don't want to see sad Zach eyes. I rub a hand across my face. Nze would have advice, for sure. But I need to figure this one out on my own.

"This is all so good," Nze says. "Your mom's fun, and *this guy*." She head-points to Liam and shakes her head. "*And* we're almost to the beach! I'm set so I can write all night if I want to." She goes in her bag, pulls out her flashlight and notebook, then tucks them safely back inside.

As usual, when Nze's in her own head, I don't need to say anything. She looks out the window, and I know she's waiting for a glimpse of the water. My thoughts go to Marley first. I want things to be different between us. I know that just because I made friends with Nze and Joelle doesn't mean Marley and I will suddenly be friends. It seems weird that I'd be different with her now that she's dating a girl. But still. There's something old in how hard it's been between us. Something I don't want anymore.

I'm thinking how I have no idea how to make things better with

Marley when the music in the car snaps off. We're parked. Roxy catches my eye in the rearview. "Come with me for a sec, first," she says. "There's something I want to check."

"'Course," I say.

The lot's full of cars. There's old-time jazz music playing and the twinkly outside lights are on full blast. I think about Zach, who's probably in there, waiting for me.

"So . . . *Liam*?" Roxy asks, when we're out of earshot of the car. "Is he too much? Am I crazy bringing him here?"

I take a second to mentally catch up. "Rox . . . it's fine. You really like him, right?"

"Well, *you know, who knows, you know? I don't know. . . .*"

We laugh.

"Nze'll help," I say. "As long as she doesn't blow him off. She's not all that reliable."

Roxy perks up. "No?"

"Shut up," I say. Now that we're so close, I've changed my mind about getting advice—at least on part of the Zach problem.

"Tell me what to do about Zach," I say. "He's gonna want to be all . . ." I struggle a second, figuring out our couple name. "*Clack!* Our couple name's Clack! If your couple name's that bad, it's gotta be a sign!"

Roxy shrugs. "I mean, it's not like you're gonna be in New York much longer," she says. "So, why not go for it with Zach? I've always liked him. And now I'm an official fan of coupledom."

Which is why you don't ask a lovesick girl for advice, I think.

At the club door, a guy who I've seen around town, a grown

but still young Black guy with a hoop earring, says in a low growly voice, "Password?"

Roxy pipes up from behind me. "Snave Yelram," she says.

When I look confused, she whispers, "It's Marley Evans, backward. It was on the back of the invitation with all this other stuff about illegal booze clubs during prohibition. You know, like this is supposed to be."

"You betcha," the guy says, staying in character. "You folks know the rules? Drink at your own risk. Cops show up, you down what's in your glass and stash the bottle. They ask, you're here for a nice dinner. Capisce?"

"Uh—capisce, capisce!" Liam says, looking way excited.

The guy jabs a thumb at the door, and we walk in. It's low-lit and we stand in a knot, getting our bearings. I can tell right off, Marley's done it again. The place smells like fried chicken and homemade waffles. A big crowd's dancing in the middle of the floor. As my eyes adjust, I see tables with red-and-white-checked cloths surrounding the dance floor. The live band plays in one corner, and there are stations where people are playing games in the others. The soft flickering lights come from candles set up on stands around the room and on the tables.

"Nice," Nze says. "Just enough light so I won't land on my ass." She points to the open glass doors at the back of the room. "The beach is through there, right? You wanna go look?"

"That part's later," I say. "Come on, let's . . ."

But I'm not sure where to go. My eyes search the crowd for friendly faces. Marley's family's everywhere, as usual, her cousins heating up the dance floor and her million aunts wearing "favorite aunt" tiaras.

A hot-orange sequined flapper dress catches my eye. It's Marley, and the dress is hugging curves I never knew she had. She's even got a little sequined cap, instead of a flapper band. But that's not even the wild part. Marley and her orange-covered curves are pressed up against a tall, dark-skinned girl I never saw before.

I gape at them because the girl—Maya—is *hot*. Marley sees me, and there's pride and stubbornness in the set of her smile. Roxy guides us to the double doors at the back of the room. The music's softer on the deck, but there's voices and laughter. I breathe in the damp air and ask myself why I care if Marley Evans has a hot girlfriend from some other school. I have a guy. Even two. Do I really not want her to have someone, too? But it's not that. It's that Marley Evans just upped her cool factor about a thousand percent.

I remind myself I'm going to do better with Marley. I do *not* want to be that person.

"This is . . . *wow*," Nze says in a shocked kind of whisper, her eyes on the ocean, twenty yards across the sand. She moves toward it like she's being pulled. Right that second, Zach lands in front of us. Literally. He's riding some kind of bouncing stick, and he jumps off neatly.

"Pogo stick," he says. "I guess they were big in the nineteen twenties."

He's got on an old-time newsboy outfit, with a short-sleeved shirt, knee-length pants, a string tie, and a cap.

"That's good," I say, nodding to the clothes. Even his shoes look right.

"You know our aunts," he says. "They've been making us get ready for months."

Of course they have.

"I'll leave you two to it," Roxy says, walking away. Zach cocks his head to the old boathouse, and I nod. The party noises die away as we head down the deck stairs. When we hit the sand, I take off my heels, and my feet sink into the cool grainy dampness.

Zach leans against the chipping paint on the boathouse and slides to the sand. I do, too, shivering a little in my slips. Marley's got torches out here, stuck every few feet in the sand. The light flickers on Zach's face.

"Slaying with that costume," Zach says.

"I just let my mom have at it," I say, and he smiles.

"I have an idea," he says. "What if we play two truths and a lie? When it's your turn, you say three things, and the other person has to decide which of the three is the lie. So, I could say, it's summertime, we're at Marley's party, and my name is John Smith. Get it?"

"Sure . . ."

"Okay, I'll go first," he says, rubbing his hands together. My statements are: *Zach likes Clae. Clae likes Zach. Zach and Clae are good together.*"

"So sketchy!" I say, sort of liking where he's going.

"Are you playing or aren't you?" he asks. "Which is the lie?"

I think about it. "You want me to say there is no lie."

"It's not about what I want."

"Fine," I say. "There is no lie."

"Great," Zach says, pretending the answer's no big deal. "Since I cheated, and there wasn't a lie, I have to go again."

I shake my head and let him keep going.

"Okay, this time, my statements are: *There's somebody else Clae likes. There's nobody else Clae likes. It's not about whether Clae likes somebody else.*"

"Ah, jeez," I say. "Zach . . ." Does he already know something about Bolt? I wonder. Am I that obvious?

"Can you answer?" he says.

"The middle one's the lie," I admit.

Even in the torchlight I can see his smile fade.

"Remember," I say. "There's two truths—that means the third one's true, too. It's not about whether I like somebody else."

"A guy in New York?" he asks.

"Yeah. It's not a big thing . . ."

"So, what's it about, then, if it's not about him?"

I think about what Roxy said about *coupledom*. How do I explain that that's the main thing, now. Way more than how hard Zach tries or how obvious we are, or even that I like Bolt, too. I just don't want to be *coupley* right now. There's too much else to figure out about being me.

"Can I take my turn at the game?" I ask, after a while.

He says to go ahead, and I say, "*Clae likes Zach. Clae likes her space. It's hard for Clae to have her space, if Clae and Zach are together together.*"

Zach considers a minute. "No lie?" he asks.

"No lie."

Zach shakes his head. "I don't get it!" he says, apparently giving up on the game. "How am I crowding you, exactly?"

I face him. "Why did you have to ask me to the party? We are what we are, and we were both gonna be here anyway. Why couldn't we leave it at that?"

"I thought it was romantic," he says. "Here's where I fell for you when we were just kids. Right here at one of Marley's parties."

Damn. It is romantic.

"I'm glad you fell for me," I say. "And I . . . fell for you, too, okay? Can't we just go with that?" I feel so at home on this beach with him. I get a juju-clear thought. Zach will always be a part of this place. And that will keep us connected.

"I guess," Zach says, putting an arm around me.

"Whatever happens, I'll never be half of 'Clack,'" I say, referring to our awful couple name. He takes a second to catch on.

"Right," he says. "Deal."

TWENTY-FIVE

THE CHRONICLES OF
CLAE AND MARLEY

Zach and I pass the pogo-stickers and slide through the double doors, back into the party. Mom's here now, looking stunning in a silky plum-colored skirt and top, her hair curled in a bob and a plum-colored flower behind her ear. I'm actually considering going over there when Rox comes up behind me.

"You spotted what's over there yet?" she asks.

I lift my head as she points to one of the game setups in the closest corner. People are standing around a tall round table with drinks on it. It's easy to spot Marley and the hot girl, and Nze and Liam. One of Marley and Zach's cousins, Anton, seems to be in charge. We watch as he spins the tabletop and, when it stops, signals for people to pick up their glasses and drink. A second later, he staggers backward, grabbing his throat, and everybody laughs.

Marley, who's next to him, takes the empty glass out of his hand.

"Bootleg roulette," Roxy says. "You have to down whatever drink lands in front of you, which might be something normal, like Coke or lemonade, but if you get the "bullet" drink—like the bullet in the gun from Russian roulette—then you're drinking pickle juice and gin. The parents think it's just pickle juice," she says. "But I got it a few minutes ago. A couple of those and you'll be messed up."

Marley and her girl have their arms linked together as they play. The girl looks a little older than us. I can't help it—I don't get how Marley snagged her. And I know it's bullshit to not get it.

"Come on," I say to Roxy and Zach.

On the other side of the room, we find a jacks game that Marley's little sister is trying to get people to join. "My mom says even grown-ups played back in the old days," she tells us. "Because there wasn't that much to do."

We sit cross-legged on the floor and have fun for a while. Eventually, the band slows down and people start moving toward the tables or out to the deck. Nze and Liam come over and slide down next to us. One of Marley's uncles comes around with plates of food, and we push back against the wall, plates on our laps, to eat.

"Not to blow your shit up," Nze says, devouring her blueberry cobbler before bothering with the main meal. "But you said your town was *dull*?"

"We don't do this every night," I say.

The five of us stay put until Marley's aunt May gets on the microphone, pretending to be the hostess of Pod's and Jerry's. She tells us next week's password to get into the club—*M E seventeen*—and reminds us that unlike the other speakeasies on Swing Street, Pod's and Jerry's uses quality liquor, not bootleg gin that's half turpentine. There's a laugh from the gin-and-pickle-juice crowd. Marley's aunt announces the prizes for best costume and highest pogo-sticker, and since Marley's family's not allowed to win, Roxy gets a costume prize and Jeremy from our class wins for pogo-sticking. When the band starts again, the grown-ups and little kids start packing it in so the rest of us can head outside.

The *real* party's about to start.

"You really want to sit this close to the water all night?" I ask Nze, a few hours later. "I don't think it's even safe."

She's yards closer to the water than where the rest of the party's set up, with pit fires and snacks and sleeping bags grouped together around Bluetooth speakers. There's somebody on duty in the yacht club to keep the bathrooms open. But no more parents or bands or games. It's so late, the fires have mostly gone out. The sound of snoring rides the breeze.

"I'm good," Nze says, pulling her sleeping bag closer around her. "So good. Go lay down." She turns a peaceful smile on me. "Thank you."

Instead of going to lay down, I head back to the club to pee. The light in the party room's cold and whitish now, from four bare bulbs hanging in the corners. Just when I get to it, the bathroom door opens. And Marley Evans comes out. She's smiling as she looks around to get her bearings. She sees me, and the smile slips.

"Oh."

She's wearing birthday beachwear now; brown velvety sweats and a gold knit cap over her freshly straightened hair. She waves an arm to show that the bathroom's free. I don't go in. If we're going to be this close and by ourselves, I want to do the thing. I want to fix things between me and Marley Evans, or at least know how bad they are.

"Maya seems nice," I say.

She studies me.

"What?" I ask.

"I saw you when you came in," she says.

"I was just surprised when I came in. You never said . . ."

Her eyes bulge. "Why would I tell you when you never want me to have anything?" she asks.

"Really, Marley? What's that supposed to mean?" My resolve to change things is in the toilet.

"I tried to be friends, Clae. But you've been a *b* to me ever since we were seven years old."

Somehow, we've moved closer together. We're squared off.

"You never tried to be friends!"

Her eyes dart out toward the beach, like they're reaching for someone. Someone who she's just talked to about this. Maya! Her new Black-*girl friend* girlfriend.

Her next words are an angry whisper.

"Black History Month. Second grade. I was going to do a thing about your name."

"You were . . . *what?*"

"Nobody knew you were named for Rosa Parks, so I was gonna

tell about it. It would have been good for *both* of us, but you had to compete with me and get them to pick your stupid dance." Her voice breaks a little on the word *both,* and I feel totally blindsided.

Most people don't know my real name's McCauley, let alone that I was named for Rosa Parks's middle name. But, of course, Marley would know because my mom would've told her mom.

"Why would you do that?" I ask, because I honestly don't get it. Marley juts out her chin, letting me know she's not backing down from her truth.

"I felt proud of you. And I thought it might make us friends."

"Oh." *Okay* . . . I try to rally. I'm not forgetting all the crap she's done to me because of one weird idea in second grade. "Well, do you remember telling me I couldn't be in your Christmas pictures in *kindergarten*? Do you remember rubbing all your presents in my face whenever you had a stupid family party?"

A pout takes over her face, but only for a second. The new bolder Marley fights her way back.

"Allisha Gant's sixth-grade sleepover!" she spits. "You dared me to lie down in the middle of the street!"

"We all did stupid dares, that was the point!"

"Yeah, but *you* asked *me* to lay in the street. You could have cared less if I died, and you let everybody know it." She's yelling now, and she looks around again to make sure we're still alone. There are tears in her eyes.

"You weren't gonna die, Marley," I say. "We weren't *that* dumb. We were watching for cars."

She doesn't say anything, and I know it's my turn to throw

something out. But, how do you say, *The time your dad chaperoned our fourth-grade field trip?* Or, *every time one of your aunts hugged you in front of me?* I hate what's happening. A lot. I don't let my own tears past my throat, though.

Marley seems to decide that the contest's over, and she won. Her chin lifts another fraction. Then, like she's sealing the deal on her victory, "I *have* friends, you know. Good ones. We're not flashy, but we're solid. And my *friends* always knew I liked girls."

We have a last minute stand-off, the two of us a foot apart under the harsh light of the empty yacht club. Years of hurt wrapped around each of us, tying us together. Then, she brushes past me and disappears through the double doors.

I feel like dog shit. Shocked dog shit. Did I know Marley was *that* mad at me? That hurt? No, I didn't. I was all about my own hurt—which is the way it works, right? I'm in my feelings and she's in hers. But then, this is what we get.

I don't know what to do with myself, so I go back outside without peeing. Roxy and Liam are kissing, with their sleeping bags smushed together. Nze's still in her zone, and Zach's not around. I pull my sleeping bag closer to Nze's, but not close enough to bug her. I lay down and stare at the stars.

At some point, Zach shows up, still messed up from the fireside round of bootleg roulette. I don't let him in my bag, but we hold hands as he falls asleep. My eyes are dry and gritty from tiredness when Nze comes and lays her bag right next to mine.

"I did it," she says. "I saw the sun come up over the water."

"Did you decide anything?" I ask.

"Every minute," she says. "I decided to keep on watching."

We agree we're ready to go, and Roxy drives us home under a still-pink sky. Nze and I don't talk as we climb the stairs to my room and fall into bed. It feels like I just lay down when I realize I'm awake again, dazed and dizzy. It's almost dark again, and the house is quiet. Next to me, Nze's out cold.

I drag myself to the bathroom. By the time I get back to my room, I'm for-real awake. Nze's still out, and Mom's car's not in the driveway. Orange sunset warms my window as I sit down at my desk. I let the conversation with Marley come back.

You told *me* to lay in the street! I've never seen her look so fierce. And I get it—why I, of all people, shouldn't have done that to her. Because we're Black, we're . . . community. And that's supposed to be what I want, right? What feels so good when I'm with Nze and Joelle, when I go to 2200 Flatlands. To be part of something . . . but, am I supposed to go there even with somebody who irritates me, like Marley?

Oh shit. Do I owe Marley Evans *an apology*? I mean, she'd owe me one, too, but . . .

I look over at Nze for help, and she snores at me. Still, I get an idea. Could I haiku Marley? Say a lot in a few words, Nze style. And maybe I'd feel better, if not good. Like I'd made a start.

I write awhile in one of my notebooks, and it's honestly not that hard. I type my best shot into my phone.

> Jealousy's a lot
> I didn't really see you
> What if we messed up

214

What the hell. I hit send fast and throw the phone on the desk, trying not to think about what she'll say back.

The stack of mail Mom mentioned is on the desk. I open the nine-by-twelve envelope, trying to remember what program I applied to in Washington, DC. There's more in the envelope than I expected, so I turn it over to empty it on my desktop. Out on my desk fall: a white envelope addressed to me, a folded sheet of notebook paper, an old photograph, and a tiny clay bear folded in tissue paper.

Marley Evans is suddenly the last thing on my mind. I open the envelope first.

Dear Ms. Mitchell,

Enclosed you will find the last articles of your uncle, Wendell Mitchell. He spoke of you a lot in the last days before he left us to visit your family. We didn't find the box containing the enclosed items until we were cleaning out a recreational section of the nursing home and discovered them in a closet. They were clearly marked to be given to you.

If you have any questions, my cell phone number is below. Please contact me there and not at the facility. I am also mailing this from my home address, since it is not going to Mr. Mitchell's official next of kin.

Maureen Barley, LICSW

I read it twice before looking at everything else. The photograph is old but clear, and I'm scared to look at it closer. I unfold the sheet of notebook paper. Uncle Wendell's careful crooked writing looks back at me.

Dear Clae,

Did you ever know it was my idea to call you Clae? Clay can change shape, bend when it needs to, but it stays strong and whole. I always loved clay.

Funny we call you Clae and your dad River.

Your mom never wanted me say nothing to you, so bad she didn't let me visit too much. But some things I have to say. Now, anyhow.

River was a good man. Solid in his own way, that's something you should know. All what happened before you were born, it's hard to understand. But it's good to try. That's your old uncle's advice.

I've been wanting to give you this picture for a long time. And I made the bear myself.

Love you.

Uncle Wendell

I look over at Nze, at the door, then out the window. Mom's car's still gone. Slowly, I pick up the photograph. Mom's in it, looking young and pretty. Almost relaxed. It's a party scene, so there are a bunch of people in the background, food tables, a cake. But mom's up front, smiling for the camera with another woman. There's a guy just behind her. *My dad.* His face is a little blocked because he's about to eat a bite of something, but it's definitely him.

My eyes travel back to the woman next to Mom. There's

something familiar. I take her in, and my hand flies to my mouth. She looks like the woman in the flowery skirt that we saw at 2200 Flatlands. Going into apartment 22.

Unless I'm wrong. . . . It's an old picture.

Thoughts come at me in waves that I want to wash over me, but I know I have to absorb. If the woman in this photograph, *with my mom and dad*, all those years ago—If *that* woman was at 2200 Flatlands. And if that woman knew my mom and dad, and she's been giving me money ever since . . . then there's a lot more going on than some foundation thinking I'm smart. She's the FGS, and she's family. And my mother's known it all along.

I flip the photo over, and there, in Uncle Wendell's shaky writing: *River, Asha, and Bobbi.*

Funny we call you Clae and your dad River.

And . . . Bobbi?

I clutch the little clay bear, sucking back tears so I don't mess up the photo. But maybe I got it wrong, I think, glancing out the window again.

"What happened?" Nze asks. The mattress creaks, and I know she's getting up. I gesture toward the stuff on the desk. She picks up the letter, reads it fast, then moves on to the old photograph.

"Wait," she says. "Clae . . . I've seen that woman, the one next to your mom. I've seen her *twice*." She holds the photograph, pointing. "That day at the Checkerboard Bistro. I noticed her because she had these hot African earrings. Then I saw her again when I was up onstage, at *SIX*. She was in the row right behind ours."

My heart sinks into my stomach as Nze claps her hand to her mouth, just like I did. "She's what's-her-name, isn't she? *R. Taylor Rose*. Who sent Angus? Who got us the *SIX* tickets? It has to be her, because she knew we'd be at all those places!"

So much for my maybe getting it wrong. If this woman was at the restaurant and the play *and* with my mom all those years ago, there's no question.

"It's her," I say. "The FGS. Years ago with my mom—"

A sound breaks the quiet of the room: Mom's car, pulling into the driveway. The lights cast their beam across my desk. Nze and I look at each other. Talk about a deer in the headlights.

"Your mom's home," Nze says, like maybe saying it out loud will help us know what to do.

My mom, who's been lying to me my entire life. . . .

The car door shuts, and a few seconds later, the front door opens.

"Girls?" Mom's voice is excited. Her footsteps move up the steps. There's a knock on the door. "Clae Baby? I went by Stromboli's, picked up your favorite. Mixed green salad and pasta carbonara should be ready in five!"

It's the Clae Baby that gets me. . . . It makes me so mad. And I want to go with being mad before it turns to sadness or something worse. I make up my mind and head for the door.

Mom's already turning away when I open it. She double-takes when she sees my face. There's a version of me I never met standing in the doorway, super calm and super detached.

"What's wrong?" Mom says.

"Nothing," I say. "You need help setting up dinner?"

218

Her eyes rake my face. "No . . . you girls just come down when you're ready. If . . . you sure you're okay?"

I nod and close the door.

"That was a little scary," Nze says.

"I'm not telling her anything," I say. "Not until I'm ready. Or maybe I'll be like her, and I'll never be ready." I go over to the desk, scoop up everything from the Uncle Wendell package, and place it carefully in the knapsack I brought from New York.

"So, we're gonna act like you never saw any of that?"

"One hundred percent," I say. "I have to think before I'm ready to deal with her."

When we get downstairs, though, the detached part of me is still super pissed, and it has ideas of its own.

"Remember when we were on Flatlands Ave., Nze?" I say, once everybody's chewing. "And there was like a river there? Who'd expect that in New York?"

Mom's head jerks up. She and Nze say at the same time, "*What?*"

"Or was it Flatbush Ave.?" I say. "*Flat* . . . something, I can't remember."

Nze stuffs her mouth with another bite, but Mom puts down her fork.

"Clae, what is wrong?"

"Hmm? Nothing! This is delicious. You even toasted the garlic bread when you got home, didn't you? It's nice and crispy."

Mom stares at me, but she doesn't say anything else. I'm still mad, but messing with her gives me enough satisfaction that my racing heart calms down to a steady thudding. Nze comments on the food, and Mom gets up to get more salad dressing, stealing another look at me over her shoulder.

I just have to get through tonight, I tell myself. *And then I can figure out what to do.*

TWENTY-SIX

JACKPOT

"Come on, wake up! And keep quiet, we can't wake Chaz." Joelle's voice comes at me from far away.

I sit up, my neck sore from the cramped corner of Chaz's car. "Where are we?" I ask. It doesn't feel like the car's moving. "Are we back in New York?"

We hadn't been in the car long before I fell asleep, exhausted from seeing Uncle Wendell's package, then dealing with Mom. And finally getting Joelle and Chaz to rescue us, sneaking out of the house at 4:00 a.m. to meet them on the corner, and leaving Mom a note that I was fine—just needed to get back to my new life.

"Hush!" Joelle says. "We're in who-knows Connecticut, making a quick stop while Chaz gets some sleep. Just come. And shake Nze, will you, she's still snoring!"

I hear the click of my door opening, then feel my legs being pulled from under me, into warmer, outside air. Joelle leans past me, and hisses at Nze.

"Will they have coffee?" Nze mumbles from somewhere behind me.

As the fresh air hits me, the memories come back. Uncle Wendell sending me the truth from his grave. Mom giving me nothing but lies. Angry Clae coming out over pasta carbonara.

We shut the car doors softly, and Joelle hustles us away. It's the purple gray of sunrise. We're in a parking lot. The only building in sight is big and lit up.

"We're going to a hotel?" I ask, wondering how we're going to afford it, but ready for a bed. "But how come Chaz isn't—"

"It's a casino," Joelle says, still hustling us toward the front door. "It wasn't far out of our way, and I need another shot at getting my dress money."

Nze quits walking and turns to the car. "Chaz doesn't know about the dress money?"

"Of course he does! He came with me to Atlantic City, didn't he? And we don't keep secrets like that." Even she must get how that sounds when we just snuck out of a car in the middle of the night while he was sleeping.

"Okay," she adds, "sometimes we do, but it's not because of the money. He doesn't care that I spent the two grand. I could get married in my footie pajamas and Chaz would be fine with it. That's the thing. He thinks I'm being extra. He doesn't get why it has to be *that* dress. So, stopping here is perfect. He sleeps through everything. As long as we don't make noise when we get back in, he'll never know we were here."

I'm with Chaz on this one, the big deal of that dress is lost on me.

Joelle pulls the door open and we're smacked with a whole indoor universe, so bright at this hour that it pushes everything else from my brain. There are shops for jewelry and clothes and travel stuff. Most of them are closed, but a few people wander down the white tile floors. Joelle has her arms linked in ours as she leads the way, following signs for the casino.

Along the hall, there are stands that pay tribute to the Native American tribe that runs the place. Joelle doesn't slow down, though.

"I got a whole breakfast setup," Joelle says. "Over here."

Joelle pulls us to the wall just beside a wide doorway, where we can see neon machines lighting up aisles of milling people. We sit on the floor against a wall, and Joelle opens her backpack. She's got the thermos, cups, and toasted bagels stuffed with cream cheese. They taste so good after crying and driving and uncomfortable sleeping. I lean against the wall, close my eyes, and think about nothing but the strong hot coffee and the creamy cheese and crunchy bread. Even Joelle's in the zone until her bagel's half gone. Then, she refills our cups and gets to business.

"So, last time," she says. "Chaz and I won enough to buy something at David's Bridal. But—I can't do it. I just know, when I show up in the exact right dress for me, my mom and sister will get that I know what I'm doing." Tears well in her eyes. She shakes her head fast to get rid of them.

"We get it," Nze says.

Joelle plasters on a fake smile. "Okay, I'm all done, so I'll get us set up while you finish."

I don't know what she means by *set up*, but she's back quick with a wad of bills in her hand.

"It's gonna be so good!" she says. "I feel lucky!" We throw out our trash, and Joelle leads us through the casino door. It's a huge room, purple-lit, like nightclubs in the movies, except the light comes from machines that line every inch of the walls, with names like Wheel of Fortune, Wild Frontier, Fortune Gong.

"I read that the ones in front are supposed to be best," Joelle says, "because then everybody out here—like when it's busy—can see, and then more people go in and try. So, let's stay close to the door, and just walk around till one of the machines calls to you."

Nze wanders a couple of rows in, stands in front of one machine and then the next. I know she's thinking that this is like a bonus for her list, even though she didn't put it on there. She puts her hand on a machine called Casino Royale in bright yellow letters against dark fluorescent blue.

"This one," she says.

"Perfect!" Joelle runs over and hands her a stack of fives. "When you're ready, press the button. We're doing fifty cents per, but it's twenty-five credits to a spin, so it's twelve-fifty a bet. Okay, when you're ready, just do it." Nze sits on the seat in front of the machine and shakes out her arms.

224

"Press a button?" I say, checking out the row of square buttons at hand level. "That's it?"

Nobody answers. Joelle has her lips pursed together, a terrified look in her eyes. I hope maybe she'll realize how dumb this is and call it off, but Nze shouts, "Let's go!" And she presses. The random pictures on the screen—numbers, pieces of fruit, thick gold bars that actually say the word *bars*—spin around and around and come to a quick stop.

"Okay, okay," Joelle says. "Can't win 'em all. Go again."

"But . . . what are we even trying to do?" I ask.

Joelle points to a red line that runs through the middle of the screen—three matches on that line, and we win.

Nze presses. The machine spins. We lose again.

It's awful, the way Joelle tries to keep her face hopeful, the bright lights showing the truth anyhow. I don't like it that she's gambling to try and win her family, and the stakes are so high, she's freaking out.

"This one'll be good!" Nze says, flexing her finger for the next press.

I grab her arm. "I can't," I say. "I can't be here. I'm going back to the car."

Joelle looks like she might cry, and I think fast to make it okay.

"No, it'll be good," I say. "Because if Chaz wakes up, I'll tell him we're just at a rest stop or something—get him to go back to sleep. You can't see the name of this place from inside the car, right? But if no one's there, he'll probably get out and come looking for us."

Joelle gets a surprised look. "You know, you're right! Okay, go. I really wanted it to be all of us, but I did wonder if you could pass for twenty-one."

"Twenty-one?" Nze asks.

"Don't worry about it," Joelle says. She hands me the supply bag to take back, and I head out of there as fast as I can. As I hit the door, I freeze at the sound of Joelle's squeal.

"See! A hit! Twenty-five bucks!"

I don't turn around.

Chaz is still sleeping when I look through the car window. I click the handle as quiet as I can, and he doesn't move. But he jumps when I tug the door shut. I hold my breath, hoping he'll settle back down, and he does. Finally, I can think about everything that happened in Gloucester.

My mind makes a door of itself and opens a teeny crack, so only bits of information can slip in at a time. I let them in slowly. In order.

Joelle and I saw the woman in the photo at 2200 Flatlands. Nze saw her in the Checkerboard Bistro and at *SIX*.

The woman in the photo is R. Taylor Rose. She is in the photo with my mom and dad.

R. Taylor Rose said she's from the Seven Founts Foundation. She said she is *not* related to me. Angus said the people at Seven Founts don't have much communication with parents.

But there they are together in the photo.

That means R. Taylor Rose has to be family, because why would you send me presents and then stalk me if you're just some random foundation person?

On the other hand, why would you stalk me if you're family? Why would you lie to me about knowing my mom?

Which gets me to the worst question and makes the door in my mind slam shut.

Why would my own mother lie to me about all of this?

The questions scream in my mind, *Why would she? How could she?* And then, I think, what if I'm still wrong? What if it's not R. Taylor Rose in the pictures, it's just a coincidence . . . ? That's why they call them coincidences, right? It's possible that the same woman was in all those places and just happens to look like my mom's old friend in the picture . . . possible, but not likely. Around and around I go till I'm in a tunnel rolling up the side to the roof, stomach dropping as the rest of me goes upside down, across the top, down the other side and up again, around and around like the skateboarders in Washington Square Park. There's no air in the tunnel, and it's making me nauseous and—

"Yo, Clae!"

I'm dizzy and I want to throw up and somebody's calling me . . .

"Yo!"

I open my eyes. I'm in a car. And Chaz is looking down at me over the top of his seat. The tunnel shrinks back into my head, and I breathe relief that it was only a dream.

"You were making mad noises," Chaz says. "Or I wouldn't've woke you up. What's happening, anyways? Where's Jo?"

Right. I sit up, remembering what I promised Joelle. "Rest stop," I say. "She and Nze needed a bathroom. I just needed to sleep. And you should, too, since you're driving." I close my eyes and hope he gets the hint. But no.

"Jo told me what you're going through," he says. "With your moms. Rough."

"Whatever," I say. "I don't know anything anymore. . . ."

"S'pose not," he says. "Sounds like your moms knew some stuff, but you cut out of there before you could ask her about it, 'cause you were so mad, huh?"

I don't love how he's putting that, but what does he know?

"Trust me," I say. "My mom wasn't gonna suddenly start talking after sixteen years of lies. Not hardly."

"Mmmm," he says.

We're quiet a minute, and I remember it's my job to keep him from getting out of the car to look for Joelle, or even to pee. With my phone tucked between my crossed legs, I text Joelle that's he's awake.

"Oh man!" Chaz says, his sleepy face still hovering over the seat back like a bobblehead. "I almost forgot! My mom remembered about that R. Taylor person. Except there was something not quite right about it. . . . Hang on, I wrote it down." He reaches in his pocket, fishes out his wallet, and starts to look through it. "Her first name was Roberta, the woman my mom remembered. Roberta Rose Taylor. So, that's a little different name. Plus, Ma says she works at a place called the Morehouse Foundation. It was hard for her to think of at first because she thought I was asking about another donor like her, but this woman's on staff at the foundation—like she's an accountant or something—not a donor."

With all that's happened, I can't get my head around Chaz's mom knowing R. Taylor Rose. "Did you say the Morehouse Foundation? I thought it was called Seven Founts?"

"That's what my mom said," he says. He types into his phone. "Yeah, the Morehouse Foundation, right in Midtown. They've got a picture of her. You wanna see?"

"No way . . . ?"

"There's pictures of all the staff on their website." He holds the phone out to me. I sit up straight, as wide-awake as I've ever been. Just as I take the phone and focus in on the photo, the car doors click open. Suddenly Nze and Joelle are here, each climbing into their seat.

"Not exactly a jackpot," Nze whispers, sounding upset.

I swallow. "I think we may have hit one here," I say.

TWENTY-SEVEN

THE NEW NORMAL

I am deep in my new routine. Crashed against my pillows in my room at Mrs. Brisbaine's, flipping through the pages of my sketchbook while Nze sits at my desk, working. Ever since Gloucester, we've switched roles. Nze's all about the project. And I'm basically haiku Clae.

My favorite comes from what Uncle Wendell told me, that whole forever ago.

> Now I understand
> It ain't right, you so lonesome
> Lies make me lonely

For the sketchbook, I took pictures of the photo Uncle Wendell sent, printed them out, and cut them up in various ways. It now has:

A page with the pic of "River" that's just him (Mom and R. Taylor WTF—my new favorite name for FGS/"Bobbi"—are cut out).

Underneath the photo, I wrote:

"River was a good man." Wendell Mitchell (Uncle Wendell)
"Your father wouldn't deserve a place in your heart." Asha Mitchell (Mom)

A page with just River *and* R. Taylor WTF (Mom cut out), next to a recent pic of me.

Does R. Taylor WTF look like River and/or me? Hard to tell.

A page with the old photo of all three of them, Mom, River, and R. Taylor WTF, taped to a string so I can flip it over and see Uncle Wendell's writing.

I framed the photo with the words *liars liars liars,* written in red, on all four sides.

"Do you think lying's in my blood?" I ask Nze. "Maybe it's hereditary, like skin color, and I'll end up like the kids on *Pretty Little Liars.*"

"You remember what I said?" Nze says. "Don't just assume bad stuff—what if your mom's lying to protect you from something?"

"Like what?"

"How should I know?" she says. "If you'd talk to her, you might find out."

"Mmm," I say. But the truth is, I didn't forget what she said. *What if Mom isn't full of shit?* It's what I want more than anything.

I shift position and move on to the next part of the new routine, scrolling through the latest text stream with R. Taylor WTF. It took about fifty tries before I decided what to say to her—without cuss words.

> Me: A screenshot of the Morehouse Foundation website, with her picture, followed by a finger to chin emoji.
>
> RTWTF: I'm out of town. I arrive in New York a week from Sunday. Would you like to meet on Monday?
>
> Me: Will you show up?
>
> RTWTF: Yes. At the Checkerboard Bistro?
>
> Me: I want to meet at 2200 Flatlands Ave.
>
> RTWTF: Can you be there at 5pm? I'll meet you at the gate.
>
> Me: No. Just tell me where to go.
>
> RTWTF: Blue Building. Apt 22.

It's that detail that makes me believe she'll be there. Four more days until it happens, and then, maybe I'll have all the pieces.

Nze turns to me. "It's gonna be really good," she says.

"What is?"

"Our project! Especially the histo-remix thing. So perfect, since everything we learned is a remix of what we thought. Do you think we can throw in some more song clips?"

"Go for it," I say, since it's pretty much all her now.

"And we should stick with the time periods we have, right?"

"Yeah."

"And practice our singing."

"Wait, what?"

"Trust me," she says. "It's gonna be great. Anyway, we still have to deal with Joelle."

I groan. The week ahead is way too much already, without a bridezilla in the mix.

"I know," Nze says. "But as soon as we get through the thing with R. Taylor Whoever on Monday, and then the project on Wednesday, it's gonna be all about the wedding on Saturday. And Joelle's gonna be freaking out the whole time if we don't help her figure out her dress."

"Maybe we should just let my mother do it," I say without thinking.

"What?" Nze says.

I sigh. "I sent her a picture of the dress back when Joelle first tried it on in case Joelle wanted to make one like it."

"Holy hell!" Nze pops out of her seat. "I know you're not feeling your mom, but that's brilliant. I could talk to her if you don't want to. Just give me her number, okay?"

"Tell her I gave it to you on the condition that I don't have to talk to her," I say. "And don't say it's mean." Maybe Marley was right. Maybe I'm a mean girl. All I know is, I want Mom to feel as rotten as I do right now.

I text Nze her number and turn to the haiku on the next page of the sketchbook.

How do I feel real
When the ground shakes and shivers
Under my spread feet

*　　*　　*

The days go like that. And then it's time, finally, to go back to 2200 Flatlands and see who answers the door. We walk all the way. Nze leads with her GPS, going on the whole time about the project.

"We could try to get the podcast produced for real, and Mr. Barber said he'd help us do it, if we want, even after the program's done."

I get that she's trying to distract me. It's just not working.

"Are you even in your body?" Nze asks.

"Nope."

"Okay. Well, I'm here," she says. "And we're almost there."

We round a corner, coming from the opposite direction than I've come from before. I see the coffee shop on one side of us and 2200 Flatlands across the street. In less than five minutes I'll knock on the door. In less than ten minutes I'll know . . . something.

Nze puts a hand on my back and guides me as if I might wander off in the wrong direction if she doesn't keep hold. It takes no time to cross the street, get let in the gate by a smiling stranger, and follow the signs for blue building. We slip inside behind some kids. There are windows open in the hallway, so that even inside it smells like summer.

I'm suddenly freaked out about the silky cream-colored dress I'm wearing, which seemed both New York–y and FGS-appropriate when I found it at the thrift shop, but now I know it's way too much for somebody I'm mad at. I wish I'd worn my glasses to tone it down at least.

We take the elevator up. Nze waits for me to knock. And because it's that or run away, I do.

"I'll be right across the street," Nze whispers. She leaves.

There's a split second when I'm totally aware of everything—my feet are on a green welcome mat, the hall smells of oven heat, the door is dark brown wood, and when it opens, everything will change. And then it does open, and a woman is standing there. My eyes search her in just the way your mother tells you not to stare at people; I roam her face, her body, her feet. She's medium brown, has on nice African earrings. It's the woman from the photograph and the flowery skirt. But other than her eyes being wide and nervous, she could be the lady behind the counter at the doctor's office, or some random shopper at the grocery store.

"Clae," she says. She blinks a bunch of times and stands back from the door. "Come in."

And then I'm in a living room. It's neat and airy, with big windows, a gray couch and easy chair, a blue-and-gray rug. There's a dining alcove off to one side. I hear the door click shut behind me.

The woman waits for me to turn around and face her. "I'm Bobbi," she says. "Bobbi Rose Taylor. You can call me . . . Well, you can call me whatever you like."

Now that I'm here, I *am* in my body. I'm in this place, which has to be full of secrets. There are photographs. A whole wall of them, and a framed quilt that could be a family tree.

I walk over, putting my back to most of the room. I'm guessing some of the photos, at least, are of family. I turn, thinking about asking. But I never get that far. Standing in a doorway I couldn't see before—but have a clear vision of now—*is my mother.*

TWENTY-EIGHT

EVERY DAY, EVERY YEAR

"Hi, baby," she says. "I'm here to explain."

Tears hit the back of my eyes. I haven't seen her since Uncle Wendell's letter. Since I saw the picture. Since *I* found my own way to this place. *And now, she's here?*

"Bobbi and I talked," she says. "And we decided it was best to explain together." Her face is too thin, and she has on too much foundation. I recognize the green shirt and black pants she's wearing, but they seem too big for her.

"Why don't we sit down?" R. Taylor WTF gestures toward the seats.

Mom sits on the sofa, and R. Taylor takes the armchair. I don't move.

"We're going to tell you everything," Mom says. "Everything you ever wanted to know. And we're going to ask one thing. Let us finish before you ask your questions. There's a lot to tell, and we want to make sure we say it all." Her eyes don't leave mine.

I see now that she's scared, and I hate when she's scared, because when she's scared, I have to be scared.

As if she understands that, too, she looks away. Her hands are clasped on her lap, her legs uncrossed, feet flat on the rug.

She starts to talk.

"It all begins," she says. "When Wendell and I first got to New York. We came because my momma died. We'd been without Daddy for a long time, our parents separated when I was small. I remember just enough of him that I know I called him Daddy. He didn't show up for the funeral or anything, and we didn't know how to find him. So, Wendell and I were alone, unless you count our sister, Avra, who's two years older than Wendell and had already left home and never looked back."

Avra? An aunt I never heard of? More silent screams in my head. But I just stand there watching the coffee table, which I now see is spread with food nobody wants to eat.

"Anyway," Mom says, "our aunt Melanie, in Manhattan, took us in. I was still in high school. Wendell was done with what passed for school for him. It was horrible to lose Momma, but . . . at home, I had to make up for what Wendell lacked, to prove something . . . I don't know. And Avra was always too much for Momma. It was better in New York in a way. Aunt Melanie got me into a good school—the J. M. Smith High School. I'd always been a good student, and I excelled there. And Melanie was good with Wendell. But she was sick, too. More cancer, like Momma and so many people in the town they grew up in. We think toxins in the water. It was awful all over again. But at least I'd already got my college acceptances when Melanie passed."

She looks at R. Taylor WTF.

"That's the year we got to know each other," R. Taylor says, picking up the story. "We were the same age, and I was so impressed with Asha. She was a force. She joined the class midway through junior year, and by senior year she was our star.

"We were both mature for our ages, we had that in common. She took care of her older brother, Wendell, and I took care of my little brother, Richard. I'd grown up knowing he was special— brilliant, even. It was such a simple truth, I didn't even bother being mad that our parents played favorites."

Little brother, Richard . . . I see where this is going. I wish I were sitting down, but I don't want to move.

"I knew what I had to do." Mom takes over the story again. "We had Melanie's rent-controlled apartment, and I worked full-time and took my college courses at night. And I took care of Wendell as best I could. It helped that I'd made a best friend from high school. She was younger than me, but she was like a sister. We even had almost the same name, Asha Mitchell and Ayesha Michelle. What a coincidence! Ayesha was smart and funny and outgoing in a way I never was. Even though I was older, she was the one that took me to parties.

"But then . . ." For the first time since she's been talking, Mom's eyes shift away from mine. "Then, when I was in the second year at college, she got pregnant. She didn't know what to do, because she didn't want a child and she didn't believe in abortion."

"*Pregnant?*" My mind stops at the word, repeats it. Lets it sink in.

"And so—" Mom says.

"Her name was Ayesha?" I ask.

"Yes."

"Ayesha?"

She eyes me, her fear turned up a notch. "We made a big deal of our names. And so . . ."

"Mom . . ." I'm shaking my head because I don't want her to say what I know she's going to say. A scene from years ago floods my mind. The summer I started at a new camp. The two of us, in the shed that was the office. Mom with a folder of documents, registration forms, immunization forms, *my birth certificate*. I saw her name on it.

"*Mom, they spelled your name wrong.*"

"*Did they? It happens so often with my name I don't even notice half the time. . . .*"

A tidal wave rolls through me. *How did I not remember that?* I gasp and clutch my stomach, but there are no tears. I turn away, lunge for the door.

"Clae, no!" It's Mom's voice. *Asha's* voice. "I have to tell you all of it. It always had to be all or nothing, baby. That's why I chose nothing!"

I steady myself against the wall. Why is she talking like we can have a normal conversation? More dry waves rack through me. I can't be here like this. But I can't leave and not know all of it, either. My back still to them, the door in front of me, I take out my phone and text *Come now* to Nze. And then I just stand there, eyes closed, trying to ignore the whispering behind me and get my body under control.

There's a weird jingle, which I realize after a minute is the doorbell. R. Taylor WTF walks past me, opens the door. Nze comes to me.

"You okay?"

I shake my head. "Ask them," I say.

"Nze," my mother . . . *Asha* says. "It's nice to see you. This is Clae's aunt Bobbi."

Another mind scream.

"Let's sit down," Asha says. And then: "Oh!" She puts a hand out toward Nze. "I wasn't going to mention this until later but, just a minute." She leaves the room, and while we're all wondering what the hell, she comes back in with something long and white draped over her arm.

"Your friend's wedding dress," she says.

"You made the whole dress already?" Nze says.

"It was good to keep my hands busy," Asha says. She looks around the room for a place to put the dress, and I avoid her eager eyes when they come my way. *As if a dress is going to make this any better.* Finally, she lays the dress across the table in the dining alcove. "Anyway . . ."

This time *Aunt Bobbi* pulls up a chair from the dining table, and they leave the couch for Nze and me. We sit. Awkward sadness settles over us like a rotten smell.

"Clae's just gotten a shock," Asha says.

240

I notice she's using her nurse's voice now. I've heard it plenty on the phone or when I've gone to work with her. Careful. Distant. "I've told her that she's . . . that she's adopted. I should have told her sooner. Now, I want to explain why I didn't."

No one says anything, so Asha goes on. I feel her eyes on me, but my head is down, so all I can see is Nze and my sneakers on *Aunt Bobbi's* blue-and-gray rug.

"I offered to take you," Asha says. "It was a crazy decision in a lot of ways, but I wanted to help Ayesha, and if you can believe it, I already loved you."

Right. Another smack to the gut.

"Ayesha was eighteen by then, and she'd gone through all the process to give the baby up for adoption. But we decided it was better for me to take you so she'd know the baby was safe. We made the switch without telling her parents. They never knew."

"Where . . . is she?" I can't bring myself to say, *my real mother.*

But she answers before I have to.

"She died, baby. When you were just a toddler. In a storm in Antigua. And when she died, that's when I knew it was up to me to secure your future."

Antigua, my mind registers. So, it was my mother there, not my father? Or both? But I don't ask. I can only say so much before I explode.

"You've probably figured out that your father is my brother, Richard," Bobbi says. "Asha told me and him about the switch, just not her parents. You should know that I wanted to take you, too. But Ayesha said no. Our parents, mine and Richard's, hadn't been good to her, and she didn't trust us as a family. By then, her and Richard had fallen out, too. And he was . . . supportive of the adoption.

"Asha was already close to graduating, and she got the job in Gloucester. We understood that she had to go, it was too expensive to live in New York without the college's support—they provided cheap babysitters, free childcare during the day. And now she was supposed to pay back her loans instead of receiving them. But when she moved to Gloucester, she decided she didn't want us in touch anymore." She looks at Mom—*Asha*.

"I had to protect you," Asha says. "And the best way to do that was to give you a life away from teenage pregnancies and disinterested fathers. More than disinterested. Bobbi told me that River—that's what we called Richard—was already cheating on Ayesha, even before he knew she was pregnant. So, once I had you away from all that, I stopped answering Bobbi's calls. And when the time came that I needed extra money—not to live, but to make sure you kept up with the other kids, all the little extras Roxy had . . . I asked for money. And I said I wanted it no strings, I'd take care of you, I'd send pictures, but they needed to let me do it my way."

"Richard was even more golden by then," Bobbi says. "Finishing college at the top of his class, being wooed by graduate schools and jobs. He was happy to go along, and it was his choice, even if I didn't like it."

"How come I couldn't find him?" The question comes out without my even meaning to talk. "I looked at all the school records, and I only found one picture of him. If he was so golden, how come there wasn't more?"

"Because he went by River on everything," Bobbi says. "He didn't like the name Richard, which was our father's name."

"And that's where the last piece comes in." Asha moves forward, to the edge of her chair, then changes her mind and shrinks back. "I knew Bobbi wouldn't put up with it forever, even if River did. So I —I lied. I told them I'd adopted you. All you have to do is put a notice in the paper at the last known address of the parents. I put one in the Gloucester paper, and sent them a picture of a fake *Boston Globe* notice. They could have checked its authenticity. But they didn't. And so, they believed that I had the power to keep you from them altogether, no pictures, no updates. I told myself that I wanted you and they didn't, so this was best."

"I did!" Bobbi says, her voice a little raised. "Love you. And I loved the pictures and the little updates I got. I really did follow you in every way I could, if you won an award or went to a program that had an online profile, I found it. And when you came asking questions, I . . . what do you kids say? I punted. I did my best to hold on to you without betraying the promise I'd made to Asha. And since I work for a foundation, with lots of rich donor types, I came up with the story. But you persisted. And . . . here we are."

I feel so much that I feel nothing. Unimportant things snag my attention, like the paintings on Bobbi's walls. African prints.

"Clae?" It's Asha. "I know I can't just say I'm sorry . . . You should know that not a day went by when I didn't question myself—*every* day, *every* year. But you were such a wonderful child, and I loved you so much, and we were doing so well together, just the two of us. . . ."

Every day, every year echoes in my mind. It's how long I've wondered, too. Known something was wrong, missing. Every day. Every year. But that's not what I tell her as I find my voice again. "It wasn't just the two of us," I say. "Uncle Wendell? Did he know?"

"When I brought you home," Asha says. "I said you were ours. He asked who your daddy was, and I told him. After a while, I realized he thought I had had an affair with River, even though he was Ayesha's boyfriend. You know how he watched all of those shows all day long? Affairs were how babies got made as far as he was concerned. I just let him think it. And that's really when I realized that I . . . I could make it so. Everyone could believe what Wendell believed, that you were mine, biologically. I don't think he ever figured out the truth. He always liked River, though. And he never understood why he wasn't around, until I yelled at him one day and told him to stop asking."

"But he didn't," I say. "Not really."

"I suppose," Asha says, and I can tell she doesn't even mean it. As usual, she's not paying attention to Uncle Wendell. She has no idea how much he has to do with all of this, because neither of us told her about the ring or the picture or the letter he left me. *Uncle Wendell*, I think. *The key to everything.*

And he wasn't even my real uncle.

TWENTY-NINE

THE OTHER HISTO-REMIX

"What I'm about to sing," Nze announces to the class, "would be the beginning of the podcast version of our article. And what you see on the screen would be in the print version."

She makes a mic out of her fists and sings to the tune of the *SIX* opening song:

> *Welcome to the show, to the his-to-re-mix*
> *Serving up know-ledge, you can't get from a few clicks*
> *Everybody knows, it's been hard to live Black li-i-ives*
> *Raising up the roof, till we hit the ceiling*
> *Get ready for the truth that we'll be revealing*
> *Nobody knows how folks self-taught all their li-i-ives*
> *But now there's arch-ives*

The screen shows the archives and manuscripts page on Black education from the Schomburg. I keep my eyes on it as much as possible, and on Nze. Anywhere but on the rest of the class, because I don't want to know if this is bombing. Nze looks happy, though, and her eyes are right on the audience.

I walked again. All the way here from Mrs. B.'s. This time, alone. It was all I could think of to get my mind out of my own problems and into the presentation. It mostly worked. After a while I stopped hearing my fake mom's voice in my head, making the list of family members I never knew I had: Avra, any kids she might have, my real mom's family—grandparents, cousins, who knows. And of course good old Aunt Bobbi and my dad. I didn't ask about him until right before Nze and I left 2200 Flatlands. I looked straight at Bobbi, trying to pretend fake Mom wasn't in the room, and asked, "Where is he?"

She didn't pretend not to understand.

"California," she said. "It's mostly his money I've been sending. He's wanted to." That was enough for then, but my mind keeps on poking at what's next. Do I call him? See him? Hate him? And what about *her*? Fake Mom? What am I supposed to do about her?

What am I supposed to do about *everything*?

But every time I spiraled out on the walk over here, the smell of coffee or a screeching tire sound would pull me back to the street. By the time I got here, sweaty and gross, I was okay. Nze was waiting with a change of clothes, everything set up, and enough excitement for both of us.

Now, in front of the class, she repeats the refrain one last time.

Nobody knows how folks self-taught all their li-i-ives
But now there's arch-ives!

There's clapping. I get up the guts to look at my classmates. They look shocked.

"Thank you, thank you," Nze says. "So! Today we'll be covering the issue of education for and about Black people, as school districts across the country remove Black history, or accurate Black history, from their curriculums."

"We'll cover several time periods," I say, taking over. "In which Black students and parents successfully fought against exactly the kinds of challenges we're facing now. Way back before the Civil War. Then the 1930s, when a Black blind woman started a revolutionary program for Black blind kids that meant they didn't have to go to segregated white institutions. After that, we'll go to the 1960s, when civil rights leaders founded a new generation of Freedom Schools that have continued all the way to today.

"We'll start with James McCune Smith. It's the late 1820s— before the Civil War—and we're at the Mulberry School in Five Points, New York, just a few miles from where we sit right now."

"Background music for the podcast!" Nze says, cutting in with the music she loves so much from the play *Paradise Square*.

"There's a white headmaster at the Mulberry School," I say, as the music fades. "But the school's tradition is that the advanced kids teach those less advanced. James McCune Smith is the best student teacher. The headmaster is enthusiastic but also problematic, and over time, he gets worse. Records agree that the Black parents and students rallied to kick him out of the school. This is a very early example of Black communities taking their education into their own hands. Records also show that Black parents supplemented inaccurate education on Black history with their own handed-down stories, so their children would know about their past."

Mr. Barber looks dazed. He might even look impressed.

We go on to Martha Foxx and how she taught art and braille and social studies to blind kids in the time of Helen Keller, but nobody knew her name. "She taught a full academic curriculum," Nze says. "Plus, because her motto was 'You learn by doing,' and because she wanted her students to be independent in spite of being blind, she also taught vocational skills, like chair caning and piano tuning. Her school, the Piney Woods School, still exists as a boarding school today, and considers itself rooted in an 'inclusive African ethos.'

"That was all very cool," Joelle says. "But it's worth noting that there were problems, too, with some of the Black-run institutions, where the administrators wanting to assimilate with white culture showed up as harshness against their Black students. One of those schools was the Palmer Academy, which was the forerunner to Bennett College, where my grandma went. The headmistress of Palmer wrote an etiquette book for Black people where she tried to get them to act subservient so that whites would accept them. My grandma says, 'Bennett was fun, but there were a lot of rules about how you sat, how you ate, even how you came in a room. It was all so we could not call attention to ourselves as Black people.'"

For the civil rights part, there's a new song Nze found that is literally called "Freedom Schools." She sings this one, too. Afterward, we tell them how the first Freedom School in Mississippi was created because civil rights include the right to learn your history and to go to schools that respect your smarts. Joelle jumps in with a few quotes we found from former students. Then comes the hardest part. We get to J. M. Smith High.

"The James McCune Smith High School," I say, "started in the 1970s as an example of a Black Freedom School. This school brings us full circle because for all that time, since the early 1800s, Black people found a way to teach their kids about who James McCune Smith was."

I clear my throat and do what I have to do next.

"My own parents went to McCune Smith High," I say. "In my mom's words"—I don't mention that Nze, not me, got the quote from her—"'Being educated in a way that honors our history, both the good and the bad, makes us whole people, able to face the world.' For me," I add, "I know that some of the history and pride my mom passed down to me is because of that experience."

That's true, at least, I think. Even if it is just part of the story.

"So, now," Joelle says, "when people talk about homeschooling, or community alternative schools, we know they're part of this history of Black people taking education into their own hands as a way to give something important to their kids."

"And we know," I say. "That we're going to keep on doing it."

Finally, we hit what Nze insists on calling the finale.

Welcome to the show, to the his-to-re-mix
Serving up know-ledge, you can't get from a few clicks . . .

There's clapping. Really loud clapping. I flush with relief that it's over, and they seem to have liked it. Mr. Barber stands up, still clapping, and tells us it was one of the most unique presentations he's seen in his years of teaching. Finally, I get to my seat by the window. And I sit there breathing hard as the adrenaline flows out of me.

Another group goes up, but I can't pay attention. I'm grateful when my phone buzzes, but I stare at the name for a long minute before I open the message. I can't remember the last time I got a text from Marley Evans. I'd forgotten I was waiting for one.

Marley: A haiku? Anybody ever tell u, u do too much?

I suppose I know what u mean, about the jealousy.

Also, ur mom doesn't look so good. You might want to call her. I can bring her something if u want.

THIRTY

DEARLY BETROTHED

"If anything could make me forget my nightmare life," I say, digging my nails into Nze's arm, "it's definitely this."

"It's so stressful!" Nze says. "I feel like I'm the one getting married."

We're behind an arguing couple in the line at city hall, waiting to get sent to our private room. And I'm terrified that we won't make it before Joelle and her mom and sister get here. I look to the corner where we've left the other part of our group, two friends of Chaz's, his parents, and three friends of Joelle who she told last-minute and trusted to not blab. Piled up around them are boxes crammed with flower bouquets, eco-friendly confetti, fancy picnic food, and Joelle's white cap and sundress for the picnic afterward. In the corner, there's an actual live-flower arbor she made us carry all the way here. The plan is that we all get into the private ceremony room, set everything up and get into position, so it's all ready when Joelle and Chaz get here with Joelle's parents and sister.

The couple in front of us finally moves, and we step up to the counter. The middle-aged white woman behind it flips her gray ponytail and smiles at us.

"We're here for the Morgan-Mingus and Prothrow wedding," Nze says. "Our appointment's for one thirty."

"Are you the brides?"

Nze and I look at each other.

"No," I say. "We're here for our friends. They need us to be in there and all set when they get here in like six minutes, so . . ."

"We can't let you in before the couple arrives," the woman says. "Your friends can get in line when they get here."

"Nonononono!" Nze's head wags so fast it looks like it's vibrating. "We have instructions! And plans! We have to set up the arbor and the altar! We have it all figured out!"

"We can only designate a room and an officiant when the couple is here. Please step aside." She smiles in a *Too bad but not happening* way and looks past us. The couple behind us steps up.

"What are we gonna do?" Nze asks as we walk back to where everyone's waiting. "Maybe we can set up, like, a little corner in here, take the flowers out of the box, and we can all be holding them?"

She gives me a hopeful look, but we both know it won't work. This is just an ordinary city waiting room with wooden benches full of strangers and peeling white paint on the walls.

"Ready?" asks Chaz's dad, as we reach our corner. He's eager, like Chaz. He actually rubs his hands together.

"We're gonna need a plan B," Nze says. She explains what happened. "It's okay, though! We just have to think of a way that they still get to—" She freezes, because Chaz's mom is looking not at her but at the doorway.

We all turn.

I know right off that the jig's definitely up. Joelle looks terrified when she catches sight of us still here in the waiting room. Chaz has a bug-eyed fake smile, and Joelle's parents look tight-lipped and upset. Joelle's got on a long trench coat over white sandals. Her mom's her exact height with perfect skin, big eyes, and a beauty mark in the exact right spot above her lip.

The five of them—Chaz and Joelle, the mom and dad and sister—stand frozen in the waiting room doorway. We all freeze, too, like mirrored reflections of them, waiting for their next move. Maybe because of my own family drama, I can't take it. I go to Joelle and grab her hand. "They wouldn't let us in the room," I whisper. "You and Chaz had to be here. I'm so sorry."

Joelle's face falls even further. She blinks, speechless.

"It's fine," her mother says. "Whatever this is, I'm sure it was going to be lovely, but . . ." She has what my mother—*Asha*— would call a highfalutin voice, low and vibraty.

"It was supposed to be so beautiful!" Joelle says. "I know it was dumb, thinking you wouldn't figure it out once we got in the building. But still, if the room had been good. And my dress . . ." Her voice catches. "I'm sorry it didn't work, Ma."

"Maybe it's a sign," her mother says. "This"—she waves a hand toward the counter—"marriage, it's a very big step. Let's just go home and . . . go at it another day." She slides an arm through Joelle's and leads her toward the doorway. And Joelle actually goes with her, looking like she's in some kind of trance. Nze and I trade *What the hell?* looks as Joelle's dad and sister follow. But Chaz doesn't budge.

"Babe?" Joelle notices after a few steps and turns for him.

"I thought we were getting married today," he says.

Joelle takes a step toward him and stops, literally caught between her family on one side and him on the other. I feel her pain. Fuck parents who think they can control everything and make you feel bad and make your whole life about them. I can't. *I can't.*

Nobody notices as I head to the line, which is shorter now. I turn back to watch the drama.

"Oh, babe!" Joelle says to Chaz. But she stays where she is.

Joelle's mom pipes up. "No one's saying the two of you can't get married. Today didn't work out, so . . . Chaz, why don't you come back to the house with us, and we'll all talk?" She reaches a hand to Chaz, but as usual he only has eyes for Joelle. He doesn't say anything, just waits for her to tell him what she wants.

"*Yes?*" the lady at the window calls out to me.

"Joelle!" I yell, holding up a finger to let the clerk know I'll be right there. "Joelle, they're ready for you. You and Chaz just have to come up and we'll get the room. Everything's set. We're all ready!"

"Oh," Joelle says. And then, like she's on a string that we all keep pulling in different directions, she takes a step toward me. Chaz steps up next to her. And it's enough. He takes her hand, and they move to the window. Nze starts organizing everyone to pick up the arbor and boxes.

"Good!" says the woman behind the counter. "Room three." She points to the door on the side of the room. "Your officiant will let you in from the inside."

When Joelle faces her parents, she looks sad, but more like herself. "Room three," she says. "Are you coming?"

There's a beat of silence. And her mother gives a stiff nod.

Nze shoves a bouquet in my hands as we walk in a little huddle to room three. The door opens, and a short tank of a Black man steps out, a big smile on his face.

"Welcome!" he says. Joelle and Chaz are in front of their guests, Joelle with her head bent, Chaz looking worried.

"Hold up!" Nze says. "We can't go in there like this. Can you two just wait a minute and give us a chance to hook up the room?"

I see what she's doing and help get Joelle and Chaz to step aside so everyone else can go in first.

"Which do you want?" Nze whispers. "Set up in there, or Joelle out here?"

"Joelle," I say. I want to help her feel strong. Nze hands me the box with Joelle's bouquet, follows the others into the room, and closes the door behind her.

"Bridesmaid time," I say to Chaz, who gets the hint and takes a few steps back. I look Joelle dead in the face.

"We doing this?" I ask. "Because if we're doing it, we're doing it right, right?"

"I hope I didn't wreck it," she says. Her fingers move to her throat, and she starts to unbutton the coat. "It feels like forever ago that I put it on." The dress doesn't have a single wrinkle. And I realize she was right, it's perfect for her. It's exactly like the one in the store, except maybe better.

"*Oh, babe*," Chaz says in just the right tone. He comes closer and takes her hand, and I pin the rosebud from the box on his lapel. Then I hand Joelle her bouquet, white and yellow freesia with red roses. It smells like sunshine sprinkled on happiness. Finally, Joelle lets out a squeal.

"See?" I whisper, knocking on the door to let Nze know we're ready. "Your gamble paid off." I'm still holding my breath, though, because it's not over yet.

The wedding room is small and square with a royal-blue rug, and a wooden altar that's covered in the flowers we brought. Nze's set up the arbor behind it, and all around it are Joelle's and Chaz's friends and family, all four parents wearing roses like Chaz.

"It's incredible," Joelle whispers.

It really is. Joelle's little sister has on a flowery summer dress with the colors of my orange tank dress and Nze's bright blue one. When the three of us take our bouquets, we look like we were made to lead a bride down the aisle.

Nze starts a low theatrical hum. *Bum bum ba-bum. Bum bum ba-bum* . . . Joelle's little sister starts toward the altar, and Joelle and I follow. The weird two-step wedding walk comes naturally, like we'd planned it all along.

We get up to the altar and turn. Nze hums a little louder, and Joelle and Chaz step from the doorway into the room, holding hands and moving in sync. Joelle's expression is fierce and proud, Chaz's excited and happy. But there's no question, they're a unit. They match in their solemnness, in how their bodies seem to fit together as they walk. In the glances they share. They stop halfway to the altar. Joelle's eyes find her mother. When her mom's face melts into a smile, the whole room sighs, and everyone seems to move closer together. The officiant raises his arms and welcomes us to witness the union of the dearly betrothed.

Now that everyone's looking at Chaz and Joelle, I sneak a look at Joelle's mom to see if she was faking. And I don't think she was. Which is why I have to fight back tears.

THIRTY-ONE

FREE TO FLY

There was so much to decide in the one week between the wedding and the end of classes. Like, my whole life. So that's what I did.

Nze and I stand at the ginormous airport window, her parents in line at the counter behind us. The plane's already waiting outside, Aeromexico in big red letters shining in the sunshine.

"It's really the dog, isn't it?" I say to Nze. She turns and rests the back of her head on the window. "The dog—what's her name again?—got us here."

"Her name is Sapphire," Nze says, fake offended. "And yeah—when they found a treatment program that has dogs you don't have to wait to be blind to get? I mean, it's a win-win. My parents get me to go talk to the doctors, and I can see for myself what they have to say. And, whether I go for the treatment or not, I get a dog."

"And because your parents are nice enough to let me tag along,

I get to put off my real life for a little longer."

"Do you?" she says. "It's not like your mom and aunt can't reach you out there. Or you couldn't reach out to your dad, just as easily. Hell, I think where we're going in Mexico is closer to California than New York is."

"We'll see," I say. If I were to look at my browser right now, the last twenty open windows would be for River Bryant. Turns out, he was that easy to find, if I'd only put together that "River" was his name. Sorry/not sorry, though. Who knows how it would have gone down if I'd found him sooner. As it is, I get to think about it for as long as I need to before I reach out.

RTWTF—the name I now like best for old Aunt Bobbi—says she told my dad everything and asked him to let me take the lead on when we talk. She said he agreed, he's waiting.

She told me other stuff, too—like that the tree quilt in her living room has bits of baby blankets from three generations of our family. Including mine. One day, I'll get those stories.

As for the rest of my relatives on my birth/real/dead mom's side, no one's been in touch with them for years. So I'll be a giant surprise when I finally get to see them. Which I will, one day. After I figure out what to do with Asha and the rest of my life.

"It's all so crazy," I say to Nze. "What if I didn't have a choice but to go back to Gloucester for this semester? What if I was on a bus home right now? If we hadn't done our project on education, I don't know if I would've thought of getting school credit just for going to Mexico and writing about it."

"This is definitely better than going straight back," Nze says.

259

She flips around to look at the airplane. "You think your mom'll be okay, though? I mean, I kind of get her . . ."

"No, you don't," I say. "You couldn't. All this time, I was looking for the truth and *she* was the big lie." I swallow a rush of sudden tears. When they're under control, I try again.

"If you don't know the truth about your own life," I say. "You never feel all-the-way safe. It's like the ground might disappear from underneath you any second. Do you see?"

"That's deep," Nze says. Then, a while later, "There's a haiku in there somewhere."

I get out the notebook I'm bringing on the plane, since my sketchbook's in my checked bag. After a few tries, I read.

> *Free to fly, way high*
> *Because the lie is over*
> *Land on solid ground*

"Not too bad," Nze says, irritatingly competitive about her haikus.

But I leave it alone. Her dad comes over to tell us we'll board in ten minutes. He's not much taller than Nze, bald and nervous. Both her parents are excited about the trip, and who can blame them.

"It's not just the dog," Nze says, watching her dad go back to his seat. "It's that I can see how it might go, either way."

"How what might go?" I ask.

"This disease. I can see—*tell*—how I'd survive it if it goes the worse way."

I don't know what to say, so I wait.

"On the darker days, I've been making myself go out and deal, so that I know I can do it. I think that's why I can go to Mexico, because maybe—I'm not saying I'm doing that treatment—but maybe, if I did it and it didn't work or it made things worse, maybe I could be . . . not completely not okay. I didn't used to believe that. I just thought, do the bucket list, that's all that matters."

"Wow," I say. "That's pretty huge."

"We'll see," she says.

We go back to looking out the window.

Mexico. A dog for Nze and maybe a treatment. Time to think, for me. Time to be away from Asha and figure out college. With the recommendation Mr. Barber's giving me and a little luck, I'll be right back here at NYU next year, in a room just like Joelle's. And she'll be here in the city. And Nze. Who knows, maybe Zach and Bolt will even be around. I'm hoping some time away will make things clearer about those two.

What's clear now is Asha can't be here if I come back to the city. In one of our text conversations, I admitted I'd gotten Roxy to go through her files, and I asked why she was looking at apartments in Brooklyn. It was pretty much like I'd thought. Asha was scared she'd lose me to New York. And she tried to convince herself that it would be okay if I wanted to go to college here. I could live in the dorms, and she could get a job and a little place in Brooklyn. She just didn't let herself think about the Aunt Bobbi part. Which I guess she's gotten good at by now. I'd had to tell her it was a total no-go.

Me: You know that can't happen, right?

261

Asha: I suppose not.

The text talks help. So many questions come to me out of nowhere, like a million anxious afterthoughts, and I text them to her. Like, in the middle of the night after Joelle's wedding, it hit me how weird it was that Uncle Wendell would have my dad's ring. I texted Asha, and she answered right away. She said River had given the ring to Ayesha, who gave it to her to save for me. She'd told Uncle Wendell that River wanted me to have it one day. Then the ring went missing, and Asha thought it had got lost.

But I don't think Wendell trusted me to give it to you, she wrote in the text. *And he didn't want to take that chance.*

I wonder if he would have cared so much if he'd known he and I weren't blood related. *People should know who all they belong to*, he'd said. Would I still count as *belonging to him* if he'd known? Or is it the other way around? Uncle Wendell was the best uncle ever, and he wasn't even blood. So maybe blood isn't everything.

I unzip my jacket pocket and slip the ring on my thumb.

"They did both want me, at least," I say to Nze. "Asha and R. Taylor. That's something. They could've given me to strangers." I twist the ring a few times. "If only they'd told me the truth, like Uncle Wendell wanted. Do you think he knew how important the truth was?" I ask. "He tried so hard to give it to me."

"Yeah, I think he did," Nze says.

We take the seats her parents saved for us, so we're all together when they call us to get on the plane. Nze pulls out her phone, and I go back to my notebook, still thinking of Uncle Wendell. He deserves his own haiku, and this one comes easily. I show it to Nze.

Uncle Wendell tried
He persisted and defied
My hero, who died

"Okay, that's good," she admits. She hands me back the notebook.

"You know," she says. "Even if you don't figure everything out with your family, we'll still have time after Mexico. And we'll have each other. Plus, I'll have Sapphire Simone. She'll be my fairy god creature."

"Better you than me," I say. "I'm done with fairies. I just want people who'll show up and tell the truth."

She's right about our having each other, though. Whatever happens, I'll have her and Joelle. Roxy. And I guess I'll have family, too, even if I'm not sure how that part'll work.

They call our flight. I zip Uncle Wendell's ring safely in my pocket: the ring that Richard gave to Ayesha who gave it to Asha, who Wendell stole it from to give to me. I smile a little at my complicated story and walk to the airplane.

ACKNOWLEDGMENTS

This is a book about friendship. First, thank you to my beloved running buddies, old and new. What a lifeline you have been. Thank you for being solid, true, and so much fun. Thank you for teaching me what it means to be seen.

Deep appreciation for my writing partner, Andrea Canaan, and the brilliant, dedicated, and supportive members of A Writer's Life. Special thanks to Amihan Matias, my research mate and book-promotion wing woman. And to my writing pals Marcia Gomes, Ellen Barry, and Felicia Bisaro.

Thank you to Purvi Shah. Your creativity is an inspiration and your flexibility a gift.

I got to know this book and these characters during my charmed stay at the Hedgebrook Writing Residency. Many thanks to the Hedgebrook staff and to my Hedgebrook sisters from both cohorts I had the pleasure of living and working with. My time with you made all the difference.

It is probably true that all fictional characters have a little bit of the author in them. In this case, Nze's struggle with vision loss reflects my personal experience. Big thanks to Dr. Kateki Vinod for her care and for teaching me how glaucoma shows up in young people.

As my own vision got worse, my fitness gurus championed the cause. Heartfelt thanks to Jamal "Marley" Morris of Shaped by Marley. Thanks for taking the time to learn about glaucoma and fitness, and for answering a million random writer questions while literally standing on one foot with me.

Did you know that you can strengthen the muscles in the arches of your feet? I learned that from Lindsay Chapman of Brooklyn Born Pilates. Thank you for helping me find my feet and to understand that a strong mind-muscle connection will always keep me grounded and steady.

I also truly appreciate my empathic coach, Ber-Henda Williams, who shared her wisdom with me and Joelle. And yes, salt-and-honey scrub really works!

Huge thanks to my publishing team: Ben Rosenthal, Alyson Day, Karina Williams, Julia Johnson, and the whole team at HarperCollins, with an asterisk of appreciation for the marvelously meticulous copy editors. And thank you so much to my incredible agent, Elizabeth Bewley, and the team at Sterling Lord Literistic.

And, last and always most, my family, Liz Roberts and Kwame Allen-Roberts. Thank you for being in the writing with me at all hours of the day and night. Thank you for your great ideas. Thank you for being home.